Her breath caught. Just as it had the first time she'd set eyes on Cesar Montarez.

He walked up to her, as fabulous now as he had been before, looking like a million dollars in his superbly cut tuxedo—lean and tall and oh, so beautiful....

He stopped in front of her. She felt faint. His dark, beautiful eyes looked down at her, rich with pleasure.

"You came."

It was all he said, all he needed to say....

VIVA LA VIDA DE AMOR!

They speak the language of passion.

In Harlequin Presents® you'll find a special
kind of lover—full of Latin charm. Whether he's
relaxing in denims or dressed for dinner, giving
you diamonds or simply sweet dreams,
he's got spirit, style and sex appeal!

Latin Lovers is the miniseries
from Harlequin Presents® for anyone
who enjoys hot romance!

Watch for more Latin Lovers—
you can never have enough spice in your life!

There's another Latin Lover coming to you soon!

Look out for him in
The Brazilian Tycoon's Mistress
by Fiona Hood-Stewart
November #2429

Julia James

BOUGHT BY HER LATIN LOVER

TORONTO • NEW YORK • LONDON
AMSTERDAM • PARIS • SYDNEY • HAMBURG
STOCKHOLM • ATHENS • TOKYO • MILAN • MADRID
PRAGUE • WARSAW • BUDAPEST • AUCKLAND

For my mother—memories of Spain

ISBN 0-373-12412-0

BOUGHT BY HER LATIN LOVER

First North American Publication 2004.

Copyright © 2004 by Julia James.

www.eHarlequin.com

Printed in U.S.A.

CHAPTER ONE

SHE looked like a tart!

Rosalind stared, repelled, at her garish reflection in the mirror propped on the chest of drawers in her cramped bedroom. She had far too much make-up on, and her long dark hair was extravagantly moussed into a stiff mass around her face. Her eyes were black sockets, lashes weighed down with mascara, and her mouth was a scarlet pout. Long, shiny earrings jangled from her lobes, and loops of equally shiny chains draped round her neck, cascading into her exposed cleavage.

She glanced down at her dress and shuddered. Slinky silver lamé, slit to the thigh, with a halter neck that showed half her breasts, it was the very last thing she would have chosen to wear. But it hadn't been her choice.

'Here,' Sable had said, 'I brought one of my outfits for you. Your boobs are bigger than mine, but it should fit you. You'll look totally sexy—and that's what Yuri'll want. He loves having lookers around him. All rich guys do. And you are one hell of a looker, Ros, even if you don't make use of your looks! Still, at least it means I don't have to worry about you getting ideas of your own about Yuri!'

Rosalind had given her assurance on that point without contest. It was the last thing on her mind. In fact, she didn't want to go anywhere near Sable's boyfriend—whose main attraction, she knew, was his wealth and the way he splashed it around on Sable—but she was in no position to refuse. Sable had come to her aid, big-time, and what she wanted Rosalind to do tonight was little enough…even if it did fill her with the deepest reluctance.

'All I need you to do,' Sable had gone on, 'is babysit Yuri for me and keep other girls off him! That lot would kill for a chance of replacing me if they could! God,' she'd groaned, holding her stomach. 'I swear I'll never eat lobster again. I've been throwing up all day!'

Now, as Rosalind stared at her reflection, her own stomach started to nip at her. She really, really didn't want to do this. Leaving alone her reluctance to go anywhere near Sable's amoral lifestyle, it also meant closing the café early and losing the tips that she counted on to boost her meagre wage. But the badly paid job came with a free room over the café, and that was worth a lot to her—accommodation on this increasingly popular part of the Spanish coast was punishingly expensive to an ex-pat like her, who had to count every euro she earned twice over.

A grim, taut look crossed her face. Money. The relentless, punishing need for it dominated her existence, making her work every waking hour, allowing her no time for anything else. Certainly no time to doll up and swan off for the evening.

Sable, of course, thought her a fool.

'God, Ros, with your looks you should be living the life of Reilly! Honestly, if you'd just see sense and pal up with me your worries would be over! There are guys like Yuri all over the place—oozing dosh and chucking it around. You could get your hands on it *no problemo* if you just lightened up!'

For 'lighten up', Rosalind knew, read 'sleep around with rich guys'—the way Sable did.

Well, that way wasn't for her. It never could be. She shuddered at the very thought. Unlike Sable. Sable clearly had no problem with living off men and paying her way with her body.

Then, Rosalind felt quietly ashamed. She had overwhelming cause to be grateful to Sable—Sable had come to her rescue when she was totally desperate. She had no right to condemn her.

Nor, she recalled as she picked up the other girl's silver evening bag and headed for the door with heavy heart, had she any right to refuse Sable the favour she asked. However reluctantly she did it.

Cesar Montarez's mouth tightened imperceptibly as he surveyed the group who were clustering around a blackjack table.

'Yuri Rostrov,' murmured the man at his side, keeping his voice low. 'Drugs, arms smuggling, extortion, protection rackets…do you want me to go on?'

His boss gave a curt negative. 'Let's just get him out of here. Give me time to feed him the usual line, then start looking visible—but not too visible.'

Cesar Montarez's head of security nodded briefly. It was a routine they'd used before. Low-key, but usually effective.

'He won't like it,' he cautioned his boss. 'He's winning.'

Cesar shrugged. 'Too bad.' For a moment he wished he could deal with his unwelcome customer the way he really wanted to—with his fists. Scum like Rostrov were not welcome at El Paraíso, however lavishly they wanted to spend their ill-gotten wealth. But such methods were inappropriate for the luxurious up-market surroundings of the resort casino. Better by far to get rid of gangsters like Rostrov in ways that did no damage to the décor.…

Steadily he made his way across the crowded floor, pausing to greet familiar and valued patrons, dutifully admiring his female guests and using his practised skill in keeping each of them at an appropriate distance, however much they might want to encourage him to linger. Eventually his apparently leisurely progress brought him within eyeline of his target.

As he stopped to return the genial hail of one of the casino's regular visitors, a wealthy, retired pro-golfer who was keen to go into business with him, his eyes slipped over the other man's shoulder. Rostrov and his party were still dominating one of the blackjack tables, the gangster giving a loud triumphant laugh as he won yet another hand, his pleasure echoed sycophantically by his entourage. The men had surrounded themselves with the usual cluster of girls, who were hanging on to them with painted nails, giggling and gasping as Rostrov won again.

The imperceptible tightening of Cesar's mouth came again. That was another good reason for getting Rostrov out of here. Girls like that were not welcome here either. The casino could do without them. Sure, he liked beautiful women to be seen here—it was good for business. Rich men always liked eye-candy around them wherever they went to spend their money. But Cesar had no intention of letting the casino become a place known to be frequented by females one step away from the bordello.

However stunning they were.

Like that one—

His dark eyes flickered momentarily over one of the females hanging out with Rostrov. The girl was a whole lot better-looking than the three other floozies in the party, with a profile that drew a grudging tribute from his discerning, if contemptuous eye. In fact, he found himself thinking to his own disapproval, she really was one of the most stunning females he'd ever set eyes on.

All wasted.

The natural beauty she had been graced with was ruined by her overdone face and hair and her totally tasteless silver lamé dress, slit up to the top of her thigh. One of Rostrov's sidekicks had his arm around her, pulling her into his side. It distorted the bodice of the dress, pulling at its plunging neckline so that half her right breast was showing. The girl hadn't even noticed—and if she had she wouldn't have cared, Cesar knew. If she cared about little niceties like excess cleavage she'd hardly be the type to be hanging around with garbage like this.

Time to get rid of her. Time to get rid of them all. Taking polite leave of the golfer, he closed in on his unwanted guests.

Rosalind tried to stop herself shuddering. The one that seemed to be called Gyorg had got hold of her, and was plastering her against him. His fat hand was curved possessively over her naked shoulder, caressing her flesh. As Yuri Rostrov beat the dealer yet again, Gyorg said something loud and admiring in his own language to him, and caressed her shoulder again.

Oh, God, get me out of here!

Her plea went unnoticed, just as it had all evening. She'd known the moment she'd introduced herself to the flashily dressed, heavy-set Eastern European businessmen in the hotel bar back in town that the evening was going to be every bit as bad as she'd feared.

But she was in no position to say no to Sable—none whatsoever.

And that was the reason she was still here, letting herself be pawed. That was why she was sticking it out, smiling and smiling until she thought her jaw would break with it, laughing when everyone else laughed, while privately counting the endless minutes until it was over.

Silently she repeated Sable's advice. *All you have to do is smile and be nice.*

And that, whatever it took, was what Rosalind was going to keep doing. Smile and be nice. Smile and be nice.

Till the hellish evening was finally over.

It wasn't even as if she was managing to do what Sable wanted, she thought viciously—keep other women off Yuri. The other two girls had made a beeline for him, and he seemed quite happy to let them—and pass Rosalind over to Gyorg.

As she tried not to inhale the sickly scent of the man's heavily applied cologne, she noticed that the croupier, a slim, expressionless man, was glancing at someone approaching the table. Rosalind twisted her head slightly to see.

She inhaled sharply, then the breath stilled in her throat. A man had come up to Yuri and started to talk to him quietly. Rosalind couldn't take her eyes off him.

He was Spanish, of that there was no doubt. The dark olive skin, the even darker eyes and hair, and the long, sweeping lashes which only seemed to enhance his searing masculinity all showed his Hispanic heritage. But for a Spaniard he was tall, easily six feet, yet he still had that svelte, almost feline grace that so many of his compatriots possessed. But did they all possess that hint of Moorish ancestry, that aquiline nose, those hooded eyes, those smooth, high cheekbones? That sculpted, sensual mouth?

Rosalind felt her skin tightening. She had seen many fantastic-looking males since coming out to Spain, but none had ever simply made her want to stare, open-mouthed at them…

And it wasn't just that he was the most fabulous-looking male she'd ever seen—it wasn't just his eye-riveting good looks that were drawing her. There was something tough about him, something dangerous, even, something that made her know, instinctively, that he was not a man to mess with, that other men would always treat him with caution and respect.

Just as women would always want him to take them to bed…

She inhaled again, just as sharply, but this time it was in shocked self-reproof. What the hell was she thinking of?

You couldn't set eyes on a man and five seconds later think about sex!

You could with him—

No. Her mouth tightened. Stop this. Right now. He's just an exceptionally handsome man, that's all. And these are *hardly* the circumstances to be thinking about men! The only thing you need to think about is getting through the rest of this evening without running away!

As she steeled herself against her runaway hormones, it dawned on her that the tension amongst the Eastern Europeans was suddenly palpable. They were looking grim. And very unhappy about something.

The Spaniard said something more to them. He was speaking in a low voice, but this time—concentrating on what he was saying, not the way he looked—Rosalind strove to make out the words. He was speaking English, probably the only language he had in common with them, and his accented voice had a compelling edge to it.

'—it's out of my hands,' she heard him say, and he glanced speakingly across the crowded room.

Rosalind watched Yuri Rostrov follow the line of the Spaniard's glance, and saw his face tense.

'You see?' murmured the Spaniard. Through the crowd, Rosalind fancied she could see someone making his way towards them. A tough-looking man with a determined look on his face.

The Spaniard was taking out a notebook from inside his dinner jacket. He spoke briefly to the croupier in Spanish, who answered as briefly, then scrawled a number with a whole load of zeroes on it and initialled it. He handed it across to Yuri.

'With the compliments of the house,' he said.

The gambler took the paper, glanced at it, his expression changing. The displeasure seemed to evaporate.

Cesar had known it would. It was costing him to get rid

of the gangster, but it was worth it—every cent. Doubling the man's winnings was a small price to pay for getting him off the premises—achieved by telling him that the Spanish police had plain-clothes detectives patrolling the casino because they suspected it was being used to launder illicit money. He'd swallowed the line totally, and Cesar didn't expect to see his unwanted guests back again any time soon.

As Rostrov nodded, and snapped his fingers at his entourage, Cesar allowed himself to relax minutely. As he did so his eyes flickered over the girl again. He wished they hadn't. Close up, she was even more stunning than he'd thought from a distance. Face on was even better than her profile. A perfect oval, delicate nose, perfect lips, and a pair of eyes that were as green as emeralds.

And as for her body…

For a woman she was tall, but she wasn't one of those bony racehorse types. She had a figure—a curve to her hip that the glittering silver atrocity hugged all too lovingly, and breasts too full for the skimpy halter neck bodice, skewed sideways as it was. Though, he mused, that did allow him to see just about all of one peach of a breast except the nipple.

As he felt his body react predictably he doused his lust. He had no interest in girls like her. She and the others would be passed around like candy tonight amongst Rostrov and his cronies—soiled goods was too polite a name for her.

Two thin lines of colour stained Rosalind's cheekbones—though they hardly showed beneath the blusher. The Spaniard was looking at her—and she knew exactly what he was seeing.

He's seeing a tart. A total tart.

What galled her most was that she knew she could not blame him for thinking that. What else would he think about her and the other girls, whose names she didn't even know, but that they were the type to hang on to rich men for what they could get out of them?

She dragged her eyes away. There was nothing she could do about the way the man looked at her—and she had no choice whether to be here or not. Sable had called in a favour and she was in no position to balk at it.

They were moving off. Gyorg, keeping his arm tight around her, followed Yuri. One of the other girls was hanging off Yuri's arm, petulantly asking what was happening. He ignored her, saying something to his compatriots. They headed for the cashier and Rosalind waited while Yuri was handed what looked like a vast wad of notes, which he counted, then stashed inside his jacket.

So much money—Rosalind could hardly tear her eyes away...

As they headed out into the vast concourse of the casino, Rosalind was aware of the Spaniard still watching them.

He must be the house detective, or casino security, she thought. Making sure we clear off. Maybe he'd been warning Yuri Rostrov that some business rival had tracked him down, ready to turn ugly over a bad deal. Whatever it was, Yuri definitely didn't want to stick around.

The chill night air hit her as they walked out of the casino on to the covered forecourt. It was too early in the year even to be called spring by British standards, let alone Spanish. She shivered, and felt Gyorg tighten his grip on her.

'I keep you warm.' He grinned down at her, gold gleaming generously in his mouth, brandy fumes thick on his breath.

His English was not good, and his accent was strong. But the look in his eyes was clear enough. Rosalind stretched her mouth in her false grimace again, and made no answer. As her eyes adjusted to the light she saw the tall, good-looking Spaniard standing by the open doorway. For a second she felt his eyes on her.

And she felt his scorn whip at her.

She dropped her eyes down to the stone flagging, not wanting to see him, and when she looked up again he was gone.

A huge black limo was pulling up in front of their party. One of Yuri's sidekicks flung open the door.

'Where are we going?' she heard herself ask sharply.

'Hotel,' supplied Gyorg helpfully. 'Mr Rostrov's suite. We have party there.'

She pulled away. She couldn't help it.

The man seemed to think it part of a ploy. He yanked her back, closer to him, his fat hand beefy and strong. He bent his mouth to her ear.

'Suite has hot-tub. We all get clean!' He gave a coarse laugh and rubbed his fat hand up and down Rosalind's upper arm. 'I scrub you all over.' He laughed again, even more coarsely. 'I scrub lovely naked body all over!'

Rosalind froze, from the top of her head to the bottom of her feet.

Cesar raised a hand in acknowledgement to the parking valet who had brought his car round, and lowered himself in with lithe grace. He was glad to be heading off. The evening had left a bad taste in his mouth. Disposing of the gangsters had been simple enough, but he didn't like the fact that they had been there in the first place. As he gunned the engine he glanced up at the wide portico of the casino. How many years had it taken him to create such a place? Sometimes, he thought wearily, it seemed like a lifetime, yet he had become one of the coast's premier resort owners in under twelve years. Twelve hard years of turning himself from an impoverished graduate to a successful businessman.

Not that the times hadn't been with him. The Spanish Mediterranean coastline was a goldmine, whether you targeted the budget tourists or those that he focused on—the extremely non-budget visitors, who just wanted to burn money ostentatiously on everything from yachts to green fees.

He nosed his open-topped car down the palm-lined drive that led through the landscaped grounds of El Paraíso, past the fork that would have taken him down to the deluxe hotel, nestling above the private beach, with its tiers of swimming pools and hideaway villas overlooking the marina where millionaires moored their yachts before coming to gamble away their money at the El Paraíso casino, or play golf at the exclusive golf club adjoining the hotel.

The resort coined money—so did its sister resort on Majorca, and the one in the Algarve. Cesar felt his mind slipping away into familiar territory—business expansion. Where to open the next El Paraíso? Menorca, perhaps, or one of the Canary Islands? Or the fast-developing Costa de Luz on Spain's Atlantic coastline? Or even on the north coast, where Edwardian aristocracy had loved to gamble away their City dividends and estate rents?

A thin smile pulled at his mouth. A hundred years on and Spain was still a mecca for northern Europeans hungry for the sun. Their hunger had brought prosperity, but at a price. The old Spain was changing, disappearing for ever. The poverty was going, too, yes, but so were the traditions, the culture, the differences that had set Spain apart for centuries from the rest of Europe once the glory days of the sixteenth century had dwindled away like spent Inca gold.

He pulled his mind away. History was a subject that would fascinate him all his days, he knew—but the times when he had once thought to be a professor of the subject were long gone. He had pursued money instead, and had done so with a success even he had not dreamed of. And now money pursued him.

As did women.

A cynical light lit his dark eyes as he headed out on to

the main coastal road and speeded up. Women had always come easily to him—especially the northern girls, who seemed to go sex-mad when they reached Spain!—but at least when he'd been an impecunious waiter working in his vacations he'd known that the main attraction was him— not what he could spend on them.

Since making his money it had been different. The cynical expression deepened as he put his foot down on the accelerator. He could still remember his first feeling of genuine shock when he'd realised that when a man made money he could have just about any woman he wanted. The coast was littered with women who were on the make for a rich man. Any rich man. Old, ugly, fat—women like that didn't care.

It had been an eye-opener, and a sobering one at that. Discovering that they found his wallet even sexier than they found him.

He changed gear and revved the engine. Well, at least he'd wised up fast. These days he was cynical enough to ensure that he only picked those women who at least provided the best packaging—and he never kept them long anyway. There was always a fresh batch to choose from, whenever he wanted.

His mouth tightened. Was it going to be like that for ever? Just a passing parade of beautiful women through his life? A self-mocking smile tugged at his lips—was he complaining about that? Most men would envy him.

Besides, he would settle down one day, he knew. He just didn't know when. In many ways it was a shallow existence, this gilded world he'd moved up into. Few marriages lasted, and the rich often seemed to flit through life like butterflies. He thought of his own parents—both dead now—and how they'd worked hard as not-very-well-paid but hard-working public employees, doing their best to give him a good start in life. They'd been ambivalent about his decision not to pursue an academic career after all. But a summer spent working for a property development company had opened his eyes to the huge opportunities that the new Spain afforded ambitious men. He'd have been a fool to turn that down.

His face shadowed. His parents had lived long enough to see their son begin to build his resort empire, but his father had worried continuously about the huge financial risk, and his mother had lamented the fact that he showed no interest in getting married. They had been killed in a car crash some five years earlier, leaving him alone in life. He had thrown all his energy, all his time, into building up El Paraíso.

His only break from non-stop work had been to scout for a place up in the hills, beyond the reach of the coastal developments, where he could live when he finally settled down in that mythical 'not yet' time he vaguely envisaged.

The cynical look returned. Of course he had another diversion from work as well—women. He never let them get in the way of work, but he certainly liked to relax with them.

He changed gear again. He was between women at the moment. His last had been a blonde Nordic divorcee, incredibly inventive between the sheets, though conversation with her had been pretty limited except when she'd tried to steer it round to the subject of her remarriage, making it clear that he would do nicely as husband number two. He'd balked at that, and she'd got her marching orders—not very happily, but he didn't care. Ilsa Tronberg had been in love with his money, not him.

She'd tried to hide it, of course—she had been subtle enough not to make it too obvious—but to him it had been crystal-clear. She might as well have been one of those tarts hanging off that gangster's arm, with a price stamped on her forehead.

A frown creased between his eyes. He shouldn't have

thought of those women. Let alone the one that had caught his eye.

A pity, he found himself thinking. There'd been something rare about her looks, something he'd have willingly taken time to explore further—had she been anything other than what she was. His mouth hardened. Besides, she'd be stripped naked and rolling around with that bunch of gangsters by now, taking them in turns...

He slowed as the car approached an intersection. Though it was well past midnight there was traffic on the road, heading in both directions. El Paraíso was eight kilometres out of town, but the distance was interspersed with *urbarijacíones* and hotels. To get any real countryside he'd have to do what he'd be doing in a few minutes—turn off to the north and head up into the hills that backed away from the coast.

As he crossed the intersection something caught his eye on the near-side pavement just ahead of him. Or rather someone.

Automatically he felt his foot depress the brake as surprise jolted through him.

Rosalind winced painfully. Though she'd perforce discarded her ridiculous high heels about a mile back, walking along the pavement in stockings—now shredded to pieces on the hard surface—was not pain-free. At least the slit in her skirt was coming in useful at last—it meant she could actually take a decent stride in the long dress. And she still had a punishing amount of strides still to take.

Fury bit through her. Not at Yuri Rostrov and his delightful compatriots—but at herself. Fury that she could have been so totally stupid as to agree to go anywhere near them in the first place. Whatever favours Sable could expect of her, joining in a cosy little skinny-dipping hot-tub party wasn't one of them!

She could feel nausea rising—and clutching fear—at the thought of what would have happened if she hadn't refused to get in the limo. Yuri hadn't been pleased, that had been clear, but she'd stood her ground. Then, throwing some kind of coarse comment to Gyorg, Yuri had thrust one of the two girls clinging to him on to the other man. The whole lot of them had got into the limo and driven off, leaving Rosalind shaken and shivering on the tarmac.

She'd started the long tramp homewards.

A stone cut into her foot and she winced painfully. Another three miles to go—and she didn't even have the price of a taxi on her. As for buses, they were long gone. And anyone stopping to offer her a lift would hardly be doing so for altruistic reasons...

The car pulling up just in front of her drew to a halt. Warily, she eyed it, automatically arcing her path further away from the kerb. She kept on walking. Don't stop, keep walking, she told herself. If he talks to you, don't stop. Keep walking.

Even so, she felt her fingers clutch at the shoes in her hand. She could use the heels as a weapon if necessary. She felt herself tense. A man was getting out of the car. She caught the impression of height, and a tuxedo. The car, she realised, glancing covertly, was a sports job.

Flash cars were not rare on this wealthy part of the coastline, and this model was the flashest of the flash. Low-slung, sleek and moulded, it looked as if it could have taken on a Formula One car and won.

Don't stop, keep walking...

'Señorita?'

The man's voice was low.

And familiar.

Rosalind glanced sideways, unable to stop herself. She halted.

It was the man from the casino. The man who had come

up to Yuri Rostrov and had made her breath catch with his stunning good looks. And who had dismissed her as a tart…

And who was now addressing her on a deserted pavement three miles from town at one in the morning.

Danger prickled at her.

She ignored him.

'Do you need a lift?'

There was an ironic tone to the voice that sent a shoot of irritation through her. After all, it was perfectly obvious that any woman walking along the main road in evening dress and stockinged feet was not doing so for the sake of her health.

But there was, of course, only one answer to make.

'No, thank you,' she said in clipped tones, and went on walking.

He fell into step beside her and placed a hand on her arm, halting her.

'Don't be ridiculous,' he told her. There was reproof in his voice, as well as that ironic amusement.

'Take your hand off me or I'll wrap my heels round your head!' Rosalind bit out between her teeth.

He let go instantly, spreading his hands wide.

'There is no need for alarm,' he said, only the note of reproof now in his voice. 'You're far more likely to be assaulted if you keep going. If you are simply going into town then I'll drive you.'

She swivelled her head.

'Why?' she demanded challengingly.

As she looked at him full on she felt her stomach lurch. Dear God, but he was devastating! Even in the dim light the planes of his face made her breath catch. What the hell made him so good-looking? Handsome men were ten a penny here, but this one…this one pulled at her in a way that had never happened to her before. Previously she'd been pretty blasé about admiring Spanish male looks—but something about this man made her think very unacademic thoughts indeed.

His mouth—so beautifully shaped—pulled in a brief, humourless smile. Whatever he thought of the girl, he could not leave her here alone.

'Well, let's just say that it would not do the casino any favours if your raped and murdered body was found tomorrow morning—awkward questions might be asked about your whereabouts this evening. That wouldn't be the kind of publicity I'd like.'

Rosalind stiffened. 'How do you know I was at the casino?' she demanded. Surely the man didn't know she'd seen him earlier? He'd been paying attention only to Yuri Rostrov, not his entourage.

The man gave a slight shrug of his elegant shoulders. 'Where else would you be coming from? There's no other place this far out that would attract a woman like you. Besides...' The slightest husk came into his voice, doing strange things to her nerve-endings. 'I recognise you. Tell me—' His voice sharpened suddenly. 'Why did you not leave with the party you came with? Or are they finished with you? The limo was big enough!'

Her face froze as she took in his meaning, and she suppressed a violent shudder. If she'd been stupid enough to get into the limo she might very well have met the horrible fate he had thrown at her. A shaft of raw fear at her own insane recklessness, at what she had done tonight overcame her.

'I finished with *them*!' she shot back.

Fingers brushed along her bare back.

'They were not to your taste, *señorita*?' The Spaniard's voice was low. It did extraordinary things to her insides. So did the casual brush of his fingertips along her skin.

Then, like a rush, caution lashed back.

'Get your hands off me!'

She stepped away, glaring at him, holding her shoes in front of her as if they would protect her from him. 'Look, Mr Flash Casino House Detective, whoever you are, just leave me alone! I'm tired, I'm fed up, and I'm a long way from home. So shove off and leave me in peace.'

She twisted away and started to head off again. But even as she took her first painful stride the sole of her foot landed on a particularly sharp stone and she gave a yelp, stopping in her tracks. The man was at her side in an instant.

'You'll cut your feet to shreds,' he admonished grimly. 'If you have the slightest sense you'll accept my offer of a lift back into town. Believe me,' he added, his mouth tightening, 'you'll be safer with me than out here on your own. Not everyone who stops for a beautiful woman, *señorita*, is as well intentioned. And besides—' there was that note of ironic mocking humour again '—you are hardly likely to get the offer of a lift in a faster car...'

Rosalind cast a baleful look at the low-slung beast, paused at the kerb like a crouching tiger. 'OK, so you've borrowed the boss's car and you want to show it off. Fine.' A sudden resolve snapped through her. Surely to heaven she would be safe enough with the house detective from the El Paraíso casino? It was one of the most exclusive resorts on the coast, and its security guards could hardly compromise their jobs by assaulting tourists, could they? And she was just *so* tired, and *so* fed up...not to mention her feet were agony...

She limped across to the car, yanking open the door and thumping herself down into the soft leather seats. She dropped her shoes on to the floor and leant back, lifting her chin imperiously.

'Café Carmen in Calle de las Americas—it runs up from the old harbour. And step on it, will you?'

CHAPTER TWO

FOR a moment there was a tension so strong it was palpable. Then, with a sharp gesture, her door was slammed shut and she could see the Spaniard crossing around the long, lean front of the car to get into the driver's seat. As he eased his tall frame into the low seat Rosalind stole a look at him. His face was set, as if he did not like—*definitely* did not like—the way she had spoken to him.

Well, tough, she thought. She hadn't asked him to stop and give her a lift—and she'd just spent the worst evening of her life. As the man engaged the engine and pulled out into the road with a powerful roar, she felt a long, silent shudder go through her. Tonight had been more than just the worst evening of her life. If she had actually climbed into that limo...

'What is it?'

The accented voice cut into her fear.

'Nothing,' she gritted, and tried to make herself relax into her seat.

She stared doggedly ahead at the road, refusing to look at the man sitting so close beside her. She could see from the corner of her eye the way his lean, brown hand curved over the gearstick. His fingers were long, with white nails, beautifully manicured. The cuff of his dress shirt gleamed palely against the darkness of his skin and the blackness of his tuxedo jacket. She found herself wanting to twist her head slightly, so she could look at him properly, but refused to do so. He was giving her a lift. That was all. He was a member of casino security and he wouldn't want a breath

of scandal attached to him if a customer—however unde-
sirable—came to any harm on the way back to town.

'A word of advice, *señorita*—'

The Spaniard's voice made her start, and her eyes flew
to him after all. She wished they hadn't. Not only did her
insides give that funny turn again—the way they had when
she'd first set eyes on him in the casino, and then again
when he'd accosted her on the pavement—but the expression on his face made her quail.

'Men like Rostrov are dangerous. Perhaps you think you
can handle him, but be warned—your life would be of no
account to him whatsoever. So, if you happen to hear or see
any dealings of his he prefers not to make public, he won't
blink an eyelid before having you killed to keep you quiet.'

Rosalind stared. *'What?'*

'You heard me.' His voice had lost not a shade of its
grimness. 'Gangsters like Rostrov don't get fussy about bit-
players like you.'

'Gangsters?'

The Spaniard glanced across at her as he changed gear.

'You don't like the word? Tough.'

'Yuri Rostrov isn't a *gangster*! He's just some flash
Eastern European businessman who's made a success of
himself since communism ended!'

The man's mouth thinned. 'Yes—out of drugs, illegal
arms, extortion…'

As Cesar glanced at the girl's face a shaft of exasperation
went through him. She was staring at him as if he was mad.
A hard smile twisted at his lips. 'Can you really be that
naïve, *querida*?'

'I didn't know they were gangsters!'

Could her shock be genuine? Cesar wondered. If that
were true then he was doubly glad he'd acted instinctively
and pulled up to offer her a lift. No woman dressed like her
should be out walking at this time of night, even if she

hadn't been at his casino. But had it just been a gentlemanly instinct to stop for her? Or had his libido been involved in that instant decision as well?

Close up, she was as stunning as he'd thought her at the casino—even if she was done up like a *putana*! But even dressed like this she was having an effect on him—a powerful one...

'How do you know they're gangsters?' she demanded, interrupting his thoughts, which were wandering off in a direction that was obviously impractical. Whether or not she'd known they were gangsters, the girl was still obviously a tart—and, however stunning she was, he wouldn't be soiling his hands on her.

He gave her an old-fashioned look. 'I know everyone who comes into the casino.'

'Of course.' She shrugged. 'It's your job. House detective, or whatever you are.'

Cesar dropped one hand from the steering wheel and reached inside a glove compartment. Drawing out a business card, he handed it silently to her. She glanced at it in a fleeting street light.

Cesar Montarez, she read. *Desarrollos El Pacuso.*

She looked blank.

'I make a point, *señorita*,' Cesar Montarez said softly, 'of knowing everyone who comes into my casino. I have a comprehensive database—a necessity in these fraudulent and financially uncertain times. Alas, some gamblers suffer from a compulsive habit that their financial situation does not support. And some, such as our mutual acquaintance Yuri Rostrov, spend money whose origins draw the attention of the police. Such gamblers are not valued customers of mine.'

She frowned. 'Yours?'

'Mine,' he agreed.

Her frown deepened. He saw her glancing both at him and at the luxurious interior of the car.

'It's *your* casino?'

'Indeed. I own all the El Paraíso resorts,' he assented smoothly.

He waited for the flash in her eyes as he revealed he was a rich man. But all she said was, 'I thought you were the house detective. I suppose I should have thought it odd that you were driving a flash car like this—I thought you'd just borrowed it.'

'No. It's mine.' He paused minutely. 'Do you like it?'

'It's very nice,' said Rosalind politely. She knew men and their cars were a serious item, and that they took offence if you did not admire them.

A laugh broke from him. He hadn't meant it to, but she'd got one out of him. He felt a wave of relaxation go through him. He didn't know why, exactly, but there was something about her total lack of interest in a car costing over two hundred thousand euros that was incredibly refreshing.

And incredibly unexpected. Most women he knew drooled over the car, just as they drooled over him.

And a girl like this one, who practically had a sign over her head saying 'Sexually available if paid', should have been foaming at the mouth for him now she knew just how rich he was.

So why wasn't she? And why hadn't she stuck with her 'escorts' for the evening?

'Why didn't you go on with Rostrov?' he asked suddenly.

She tensed. 'Because I'm not that stupid!' she retorted. 'I might have been stupid enough not to realise he was a gangster, but I'm not stupid enough to get into a limo with him and go back for a spot of cosy communal hot-tubbing!'

His brows drew together. 'Forgive me,' he said in a soft voice that made her flesh crawl, 'but I rather thought that was the object of the exercise.'

Rosalind's face set. OK, so he thought her a tart. She couldn't blame him. But she was damned if he was going to think her a slut as well as a naïve idiot who couldn't spot a gangster when she was plastered against one!

'Well, it wasn't! The reason I was with them was because…because I was doing Yuri Rostrov's girlfriend a favour. She's down with a bug, and she didn't want some other woman moving in on her rich squeeze. So I was there babysitting him—*just* in public—that's all! When he and his mates wanted to make the party private I called time, OK? They didn't like it, and I ended up heading for home on foot.'

He frowned. 'You should have asked the doorman to order you a taxi.'

'Taxis cost money, Señor Montarez,' she answered tightly.

'You only like to spend other people's money, then?' he riposted. There was a clear jibe in his voice.

'You have no call to say that,' she replied, even more tightly.

He shrugged. 'The coast is packed with girls looking for men to spend money on them.'

'Well, I'm not one of them!' she retorted.

A grim smile parted his mouth. 'If you don't want people to make such an assumption about you then you had better not hang around with the likes of Yuri Rostrov—even if he were just the legitimate businessman you say you thought he was.'

'I told you, I was doing a friend a favour!' she snapped hotly.

He glanced down at her, eyes flickering.

'Indeed,' he murmured.

His blatant disbelief galled her.

'Look, Señor Montarez,' she launched, determined he should take that cynical look off his face when she defended herself, 'I'm a naïve idiot, like you said, but I'm *not* that kind of girl—even if you have every reason to think I am!'

'Then I suggest,' he said sardonically, 'that you don't keep company with types like Rostrov in future—or do any of his girlfriends a favour!'

'Believe me, I won't,' she answered tightly. 'But the fact that I did doesn't make me a tart! So you can just damn well stop looking down that haughty nose of yours at me. I didn't ask for a lift, and I didn't ask for you to lecture me on Eastern European gangsters—though I accept that you meant it kindly. But your concern is not necessary. Believe me, I'm never going to go near Yuri Rostrov again, and I'm never going to step foot inside your precious casino again. So before you move on to what I'm sure is going to be a friendly warning not to pollute your deluxe resort, you can save your breath.'

'That,' said the man beside her, 'is a pity. That you do not intend to set foot in my casino again,' he clarified.

Satisfaction was surging through him. Her protestations had been so vehement, her obvious affront at being thought—and called—a tart so genuine, that he could not now disbelieve her.

And if she really hadn't known Rostrov was a gangster, and hadn't been having sex with him or intending to, then— oh, then the deep, powerful impulse that his libido was urging him to could finally be responded to. And that, Cesar thought, was a very good feeling indeed. He could pursue her himself—starting right now.

Rosalind stared at him, astonished by what he had just said. It was totally unexpected. He actually *wanted* her to visit the casino again?

Why?

They had reached the town now and were heading for the old port area, the streets narrowing.

As he turned a corner Cesar smiled across at her. Rosalind

felt her insides clench. There was something about the way he smiled, something about the way his long, long lashes swept down over his eyes, something about the way the dim light etched the planes of his face, that just made her feel weak and breathless.

There was nothing cynical or sardonic about this smile.

All it was, was…sexy.

She felt weak all over again, and even more breathless.

As if he knew, he said, in a voice like silk, 'I should like you to come to my casino again—but this time as my guest, Señorita…?' He paused expectantly.

Numbly, she supplied her name. 'Foster. Rosalind Foster.'

'Señorita Foster,' he murmured, and she heard the hard syllables of her name melt in his liquid accent, sending another little quiver through her.

He turned back to steering the low-slung car carefully down the narrowing street, past the cars. Above the throaty purr of the powerful engine came a burst of noise from a bar. Rosalind could feel her heart slamming in her chest, and her fingers clenched over her evening bag. This was mad! She'd had the worst evening of her life, her feet were shredded, and she'd nearly ended up in the middle of an orgy with a bunch of gangsters! But, for all that, something was bubbling through her veins as if champagne had been injected into her.

And all because of the man sitting next to her—the most breathtaking man she'd ever seen, ever breathed the same air with…

And he'd just said he wanted to see her again…

Unfortunately, there was only one answer she could give.

'I'm afraid that's not possible.'

Her voice sounded clipped. Closed. Cesar felt surprise ripple through him. Women didn't turn him down. At least not in a prim little voice like this English female. If they ever turned him down it was in a way that made it blazingly obvious that they were simply playing hard to get—part of the ritual flirtation that some women liked to go through so they could feel they weren't just falling into his bed like a ripe peach.

But they always fell in the end…

This one would, too.

There was no reason for her not to.

She was responsive to him; that was obvious. For all her indignation, the signs were indisputable. He found favour in her eyes, he could tell. It was a reaction he was uniquely familiar with. And, though his wealth now made women even more eager, he also knew that when the air shimmered with electricity the way it was doing now it had nothing to do with his bank balance.

But something far more powerful.

He felt anticipation surge through him. He would make his move on her now the impediment of her supposed association with Rostrov was out of the way.

As he nosed the car forward he glanced across at her. The dress—obscene, but forgivable now—was still showing a generous amount of cleavage, and his gaze lingered momentarily on the lush swell of her breasts. Oh, yes, he could definitely indulge himself with her! Most definitely!

Right now?

Conscience tugged at him. Many men, he knew, did not require extensive acquaintance with a woman before bedding her. Nor did many women before bedding a man. Some were happy with nothing more than a couple of glasses of wine before the greatest physical intimacies of each other's bodies could be happily enjoyed to mutual pleasure. But for himself he preferred a little more subtlety. He liked to gather the flavour of a woman first, enjoy the process of seduction, letting the anticipation mount. Both knew the final destination, but the journey there was enjoyable in its own right.

All the same…with this one…

He really, really wouldn't mind cutting the journey short…

He was tempted—yes, very tempted. He hadn't set eyes on so stunning a woman for a long time, and after having thought her soiled goods, the discovery that she wasn't gangster trash after all made her all the more attractive—for having once been off the menu.

And the sooner he got her out of that atrocity of a dress the better…

The car reached the end of the street. Calle de las Americas was to the right, but it was going to be a tight turn. He could see the sign for the Café Carmen halfway down the street—not a prepossessing establishment, but typical of tourist cafés in this part of town. It wasn't, however, the kind of place he'd care to leave his car overnight, even if he could find a space—which was unlikely, given the nose-to-tail cars pulled up over the narrow pavement. Of course, he mused, he could always simply tell her to collect her toothbrush, and then they could both head up to his *castillo* up in the hills…

Would she come? He gave an inward smile. He could persuade her; he was sure. He hadn't reached the age of thirty-four without knowing when a woman was attracted to him. She was aware of him, it stood out a mile—from the way she held her body, just so, to the way her glance kept slipping away from him every time he caught it. As for the frisson caused by him having accused her of being a tart— well, that could be very erotic, too. She might not want to think of herself as a tart—and nor did he, of course—but the accusation had made her hyper-aware of the sexual role he had already cast her in. Desire was already shimmering between them like petrol vapour. It would sheet into flame the moment he induced flashpoint!

But—should he light the touchpaper tonight? Or savour

the anticipation of deferring the pleasurable moment? Both had their attractions, but which should he choose?

'This is fine. Let me out here. You'll never get this thing round the corner.'

Her voice cut through his reverie. It still had that clipped, closed tone to it. Cesar gave another inward smile. English girls could be like that sometimes. All that 'don't touch' stuff that they sometimes put out…until you simply reached through it and touched them—as, of course, they actually wanted to be touched all along. And if this English rose didn't want him to touch, then she shouldn't have shimmered sexual awareness at him from the first time she'd laid eyes on him, those green eyes hanging on his face as he'd sorted out Rostrov.

No, it was mutual all right. And now, very satisfactorily, there was no reason in the world not to enjoy that attraction to its ultimate limit.

However clipped a tone she adopted…

He paused the car, holding it in neutral, and turned to her properly.

Dios, but she really was something! The dim light was softening her make-up, simply making her eyes look huge and dark, and the wind off the sea had taken most of the excess volume out of her hair, so that it simply flowed down her back in wild, rippling waves. She had turned to him almost fully, and as his eyes met hers he felt a shaft of desire stab at him. Oh, yes, she was aware of him all right! Her gaze was flickering, trying to move away, but unable to drag itself from his.

He smiled.

'Do you really want to get out?' he asked softly.

Rosalind tensed. Tensed even more than she had already. Something was leaping between them, had been ever since he had casually invited her to his casino again…

Some barrier had come down—the barrier of him thinking her so promiscuous—and the realisation was sending champagne coursing through her bloodstream again. The scorn that had been in his eyes when she'd been with Yuri was quite absent now. Now all that was in his eyes was...

Desire.

That was it.

She might have not dated for ever, but she was not so stupid she could not spot desire in a man's eyes.

And such a man...

The tumbling feeling came again in her stomach. It shouldn't be there—she didn't have time for it. She had much more to worry about than whether a man who made her jaw fall open had the slightest awareness of her existence as a woman.

But this was coming at her even when she didn't want it to. When she didn't have time for it. Didn't have space for it in her life. Her life was focused on one thing only—money. Earning it—day by day, week by week, month by month. Until she was free of the burden crippling her.

She didn't have time for romance.

Even with a man like Cesar Montarez, who took her breath away with his dark, desiring eyes.

Asking her if she really wanted to get out of his car...

What would happen if I didn't?

The thought took hold. *What would happen if I stayed right here?*

She pressed her lips together, trying to drag her gaze away from those long-lashed, waiting dark eyes. And failing completely.

She knew what would happen if she stayed in the car—it didn't take a clairvoyant to tell her that. She'd take a one-way journey into his bed...

No! That was impossible. It didn't matter that she was sitting beside a man who made the breath crush from her lungs, who set her blood singing, her skin aching with awareness, aching for him to touch her.

As his eyes were touching her. She could feel her pupils dilate, watched with dread fascination how his were doing the same as she went on looking into his eyes, feeling them touch her. She could smell the maleness of him, mingled with the leather from the seats, a clean, male smell touched with a heady aromatic echo of aftershave. Not overpowering, but oh, so potent.

Time was slowing down. She could feel it even as she went on sitting there, her hands clasped over her evening bag, her eyes gazing at him. As his arm curled over the steering wheel as he half twisted his lean body towards her, waiting for her answer.

'I can't,' she heard herself whisper. 'I can't.'

A tiny smile tugged at his mouth. She felt her insides churn again.

'Try,' said Cesar, and slid his hand beneath her hair, touching the nape of her neck with the tips of his fingers as he drew her mouth towards his. 'Try.'

His kiss was bliss. Rosalind's eyes fluttered closed—as if to shut out both what she was doing and to savour it more fully.

His mouth was warm, his lips a tantalising, oh-so-skilful blend of soft and hard, teasing…and tasting.

She felt weakness wash through her—weakness and sweetness, like honey. Her mouth moved beneath his, opened beneath his, and she gave a little sigh, all unheard as his tongue caressed hers, widening her mouth as he moved with slow sensuality.

Time slowed, and stopped. Stopped until, with an emptying ache, he drew back from her.

'That,' said Cesar, sliding his hand away from the nape of her neck so that he could touch her swollen lower lip with his fingertip, 'was a very good try, *querida*. But…' his voice husked as he bent his head towards her again '…you might do even better next time…'

She jerked back. Straightening like a ramrod.

'No!'

The rejection was sharp. Absolute.

Cesar stilled. Did she mean it? It sounded genuine. All too genuine.

If so, it was completely at odds with the way she had responded to him seconds ago. Then she had been soft and honeyed, breathing in his desire with her own. But now she was pulled back against the passenger door as if he were pointing a gun at her.

'Thank you very much for the lift. I have to go now!'

The words came out in a scrambled rush. They were accompanied by a jerky fumbling for her shoes, and then an equally jerky fumbling for the handle to the door.

He caught her wrist. She tensed like a deer.

'I don't want you to go.'

It was true—he didn't. Something about this woman was making him want to hold on to her, not risk losing her.

His voice was low, and oh-so-persuasive. She felt her breath catch again. But a moment later her voice came to her rescue.

'Yes, well, that's pretty obvious. But if you'd wanted payment for the car ride you should have made it clear earlier. Then I could have turned down the lift.'

His face hardened. He was angered, she knew, but she didn't care. All she cared about was getting out of this car. Fast.

'Don't behave like the tart I took you for!' His reprimand was sharp, and made her flinch. But she was panicking— badly—and just needed to get out. Because if she didn't get out of this car right now…

'OK, so it was just a nice little goodnight kiss. Fine. Well, goodnight, then, Señor Montarez. Thank you kindly for the

lift, and I hope gangsters never cross your threshold again.
I won't either.'

Her voice was breathless again, but she was trying to go
for closure as fast as she could—and then get out.

'Why?'

She stared. 'Why what?'

'Why won't you cross my threshold again?'

There was a genuine question in his voice, as though her
refusal made no sense to him. The anger had gone—but not
his hold on her wrist. His clasp was warm, and the blood
in the veins beneath his fingers seemed to be heating. She
ought to pull away, but she didn't quite have the strength.
Not quite.

'Why?' she reiterated. 'Well, it's obvious. It's not the sort
of place I hang around—way out of my league. I haven't
got any money to gamble, and I've already told you I don't
make a habit of going there with men!'

'I am very glad to hear it. The only man I want to see
you with there is me, Señorita Foster.'

He was laughing at her. She could tell. It did strange
things to her. Made her angry. Made her breathless.

She pulled her wrist free.

'Well, it really doesn't matter what you want, because
you are not going to get it! I'm not a tart—and I'm not a
one-night stand either. So there is obviously no point whatsoever in me having anything more to do with you, Señor
Montarez—either tonight or any other night. Sorry, but there
it is. I know a lot of English girls out here might act differently, but I've been here nearly three years and I don't
do one-night stands.' She took another deep breath, and a
surge of relief went through her as she finally found the
door handle and managed to make the door open. 'So, like
I said, thanks for the lift and all that—and goodnight!'

She scrambled out of the car, refusing to look at him,
trying to make herself feel indignant that he'd made such a

blatant pass at her, but feeling only that she was walking away from something...someone...that would never, ever come her way again. But then she was slamming the car door and hobbling away down the cobbled street, heading for the precious haven that was the side entrance to the café.

Like daggers in her back she could feel the car's headlights pin her, and it wasn't until she was safely inside the door, and shooting all the bolts on it methodically, that she heard the distinctive noise of the sports car's engine firing up again. As the subdued roar ebbed away into silence she stood there at the foot of the narrow stairs, with the peeling walls, and tried to work out whether she felt sick with relief—or just sick with regret.

Then, hitching her skirt free of her ankles, she started to climb the stairs to her room above the café, trying not to remember what it had felt like to be kissed by such a man...

'Cesar Montarez. *Cesar Montarez.*' The fluid syllables rolled over Rosalind's tongue, sounding exotic, enticing.

Like the man whose name it was.

As she methodically stripped the layers of make-up off her face his name danced through her brain. And the image of his tall, feline body, his lean, sculpted face, haunted her.

She felt breathless, as though a steamroller had run over her. Her adrenaline was high, she could tell, her breathing shallow.

'Stop this!'

The adjuration hissed from her mouth. What on earth was the point of thinking about a gorgeous Spaniard who had drawn her mouth to his and kissed her as she had never been kissed before? Inflamed her senses as no man had ever done before?

No point at all. The likes of Cesar Montarez, who doubtless collected women like pearls on a string, were not for her.

And besides, she thought grimly, there was no time in her life for romance. Or even dalliance.

Only for work and earning money. Endlessly earning money…

So that little by little, grain by grain, week by week, she could repay the crippling debt she owed.

Slowly despair filled her, as familiar as it was dismaying. How, *how* had she got into such a hideous, hideous mess—owing thousands, *thousands* of euros?

Her eyes shadowed, pierced with sudden sorrow. No, not mad. Not mad at all.

Her chin lifted. She would do it all again—*all*—at the drop of a hat. Instantly, without the slightest hesitation. None at all.

Slowly Rosalind went back to wiping the make-up from her eyes, suddenly wet with tears. Familiar tears. Tears that washed away all thoughts of her crippling debts, all thoughts of everything. Even of Cesar Montarez.

'Ros! What the hell did you think you were playing at?'

Sable's voice was shrill.

'I asked you to babysit him! Not hand him on a plate to that cow Lena! Honestly, I really didn't think you'd let me down like that!'

Rosalind had known Sable wouldn't be thrilled when she discovered that she'd walked out on Yuri. Sure enough, the other girl, who'd surfaced from her bout of sickness, was now sitting up at the café counter, letting rip.

'Yes, well,' said Rosalind repressively, glad that the café was empty, since Sable was hardly restraining her voice, 'the evening got cut short. You told me Yuri usually spent the night gambling, and I could just slope off when the casino finally closed at dawn. But something happened and Yuri left soon after midnight.'

'You should have stuck with him!' Sable hissed.

Rosalind leant forward across the counter, setting aside the cup she'd been drying.

'They were going back to his hotel. They were planning a spot of communal clothes-free hot-tubbing. That wasn't in the deal and you know it! So I walked!'

Sable's pretty face set. 'Thanks a bunch, Ros. He spent the night with Lena and now she's crowing about it—says she's got him again tonight! Well,' she went on viciously, 'we'll see about that! I'm not losing Yuri to her—she can make do with that oaf Gyorg. But Yuri's *mine!*'

Rosalind said nothing. They were welcome to each other—she wanted nothing more to do with them.

Except that cutting Sable out of her life wasn't an option. Not yet. She was bound to the other girl by a lot more than the fact they were both ex-pats living out here.

She sighed inwardly. She had no right to feel hostile to Sable—just the reverse. If it hadn't been for Sable she dreaded to think what would have happened. Six months ago the loan company had turned really ugly on her, upping her interest rate exorbitantly, threatening to make it impossible for her to ever get out of debt for years and years, however hard she worked. She'd been desperate.

Sable had been a godsend.

'Look, I'll lend you the money, OK? I'm flush right now and I can afford it,' she'd told Rosalind, who had been sick with worry. 'Then you can get those loan sharks off your back and pay me back instead at the old interest rate.'

Rosalind had seized on Sable's offer with both hands and boundless gratitude. But, even paying the other girl back as much as she could afford every month, it was still going to take for ever to clear the full amount. Sable, of course, thought her mad not to take the easy way out and get some rich, besotted bloke to fork out for her.

'I can't believe you prefer slaving away like a skivvy

when you could have it so easy!' she'd told her a hundred times.

She said it again, as she put her bad mood aside and cadged a cup of coffee from Rosalind.

'Didn't last night show you what you're missing out on, Ros? That Paradise place is fantastic! I went there once with another guy—I hope Yuri takes me there tonight! Once I get rid of Lena,' she added darkly.

Rosalind did not like to tell her that she doubted Yuri Rostrov would be allowed into the casino again. She glanced at Sable. Did she realise Rostrov was a gangster, not just a new-rich, post-communism businessman?

Somehow, knowing just how streetwise the other British girl was, Rosalind could not believe she didn't know. Perhaps she just didn't like to think of herself as a gangster's moll…

Anyway, it was nothing to do with her any more, and she was just grateful for that. She was sorry she'd let Sable down—but the evening had gone totally belly-up. And even gratitude to Sable for having lent her so much money when she was so desperate could not make her join in with the other girl's amoral lifestyle. Let alone go within a mile of her gangster boyfriend.

A shudder went through her yet again, which she suppressed for Sable's sake. It wasn't her place to judge Sable.

Some customers entered the café, and Rosalind turned her attention to them. Soon after Sable left, telling Rosalind she had a heavy-duty session of making herself look gorgeous enough to get Yuri back before Lena got her claws totally into him.

Relieved that she had gone, but feeling bad about feeling relieved, Rosalind got back to work.

But as she rushed backwards and forwards, single-handedly serving customers, preparing food and clearing up afterwards, she had a sudden, searing memory of sitting in a flash low-slung car with the most fabulous man in the world next to her, leaning towards her to kiss her...

A glass slipped from her fingers and smashed on the floor.

Along with her memory.

Cesar Montarez wasn't for her.

But he continued to haunt her dreams—sleeping and waking. It still seemed fantastic—that a man as fabulous as Cesar Montarez should have wanted to pursue his acquaintance with her. To see her again. To invite her to his casino.

Her good sense bit back, all the same.

And just why, my girl, does he want to see you again, pray? To offer you a one-night tour of his bed, that's all! You told him you didn't do one-night stands, and that was that. It doesn't matter than he's the most fantastic kisser you've ever known. He just wants an easy lay. Don't be it!

Her jaw tightened, her heart falling. No, it didn't matter how much her heart skipped a beat just thinking of Cesar Montarez. There was simply no point thinking about him.

Yet, even while her good sense told her that, she still found herself dreaming of him, longing for him.

The thought of seeing him again tempted her unbearably.

You could take a night off and go back, couldn't you? It would just be to see him again, that's all. Nothing else. Just to look at him one last time.

Her good sense bit back again, promptly.

Yeah, right—looking at him! That's all you want to do? Liar! You want to do a whole lot more than look—and so does he! So wise up!

She went on mopping the café floor before she opened up for breakfast. Señor Guarde the proprietor would call in today, she knew. It was his day for checking out the café and collecting receipts. He owned quite a few cafés in town, and, whilst she had nothing in particular against him, she was aware that because he provided her with free accommodation she was poorly paid for the work she did. And she was a good worker—diligent and responsible.

But then she had to be. She had a mountain of debt to repay.

A caustic smile, bereft of humour, tugged at her. She thought of the incredibly flash car she'd come back in the other night. God knows what it had cost, but to Cesar Montarez it was just a toy! How on earth had she thought him just a house detective? she wondered. The designer tux ought to have told her differently, let alone that look about him of deep, sleek assurance that only wealth could confer.

I'm thinking about him *again*, she realised exasperatedly. Can I not get the wretched man out of my head?

No—and you don't want to either! You want to go on thinking about him. Dreaming about him. Even though it's completely pointless! Even though you know perfectly well that even if you did go back to El Paraíso he would simply enjoy you for one night and that would be that.

With renewed vigour she attacked the tiled floor.

But you'd enjoy him too…

A treacherous voice from the part of her that had nothing whatsoever to do with good sense whispered temptingly in her ear.

And what's so wrong with enjoying yourself?

You can't afford it, my girl! answered her good sense robustly. The only reason you're sighing like a fool over that man is that you want to run away from what you're up against. But you can't. You got yourself into this situation with eyes open and you know full well you would do the same thing all over again. This is the situation, and you're stuck in it. The only way out is to repay Sable, little by little, the way you are doing. You can't run away, and you certainly can't afford to indulge in idiotic daydreams about millionaire Spaniards with eyelashes like silk and a mouth to die for…

With a determined twist of the mop-head in the bucket, Rosalind went on cleaning the floor.

It was in the post-lunch lull, when the Spanish were taking their siestas, that Sable turned up. Rosalind was doing the books for the café, ordering supplies and nibbling at a bowl of *tapas*. An English couple, ignoring the siesta, were drinking coffee at a table on the pavement, but the inside of the café was empty.

Sable swung in through the door, wearing a very short, tight pink skirt and an off-the-shoulder clinging white top. Her bleached blonde hair was pushed off her face with a pair of sunglasses that glittered with diamanté frames.

She swayed up to the bar in her high heels, her figure waving provocatively in her habitual fashion. Rosalind spotted the male half of the English couple on the pavement goggle at Sable through the window before his girlfriend yanked his attention back to her.

Sable perched on a high stool, crossed her legs, and set her pink patent leather bag on the surface of the counter.

'Hi,' said Rosalind. 'How's things?'

There was a curious air about Sable. She was looking buoyant, but slightly chary as well.

'Good and—not so good. Well, could be all good—if you help me out.' The other girl eyed her straightly, in a way that started a bad feeling at the bottom of Rosalind's stomach.

'What is it?' she asked, setting aside her order book. She looked at the other girl. 'Um—did you dispose of Lena?'

Sable smirked, diverted. She flicked her fingers, her long pink-varnished nails looking momentarily like talons.

'Oh, yes,' she said, with a note of definite satisfaction.

Rosalind forbore to ask just how Sable had disposed of her rival.

But Sable was speaking again, and there was a strange expression on her face.

'The thing is, Ros, even though I've peeled Lena off Yuri, it's still a bit dodgy for me.'

'How come?' She didn't really want to know, but that bad feeling was still sitting in the pit of her stomach. Sable was here for a purpose, and that made her wary.

'Well, you see, the thing is…Yuri's a bit…well…upset about the other night.'

The bad feeling in Rosalind's stomach grew.

'He really didn't like being walked away from. People don't do that to him. Especially girls.'

Cold started to pinch at Rosalind.

'Well, I did explain to him,' she began carefully, 'that I'd only agreed to go to the casino with him—nothing else.'

Sable fluttered her hand. 'Yes, well, you see—that didn't go down too well, to be honest. The thing is…' She took a breath. 'Yuri—um—well, he's a total doll most of the time—a real sweetie—but he does like to get his own way.' She gave a forced laugh. 'Well, what man doesn't? But the problem is…' She spread her hand. 'Yuri feels he's sort of—well, lost face, I guess. You know—you flouncing off in a huff and all that.'

'I don't really see it as "flouncing off in a huff", Sable,' Rosalind said, even more carefully. 'I was invited back for some naked hot-tubbing. Even I know what that would have ended up as! That guy Gyorg was all over me! And it was pretty obvious what he expected! I don't do sex like that—'

'You don't do sex, period!' Sable interrupted. 'And it's totally unnatural! Anyway, that's not the point, Ros. The point is, Yuri is definitely miffed—and right now he's taking it out on me! I mean, I could really, really do with some new clothes—I haven't got a thing to wear any more! But Yuri's playing tightwad. Basically, he's sulking—and it's because you flou—walked out…the other evening. He's making me take the rap for it!'

Rosalind swallowed. What the hell was Sable after?

She found out a moment later.

'The thing is,' said Sable again, eyeing Rosalind straightly, 'Yuri is the best guy I've had in ages! He really knows how to spend his money—and I seriously don't want to screw it up with him! But there's a hell of a lot of competition out there for him! I've really got to pull out the stops to make sure it's me he sticks with! That's why I thought I was being so clever the other night—sending you along to babysit him. I didn't realise,' she went on darkly, 'it would be such a disaster.'

'Yes, well,' answered Rosalind feelingly, 'neither did I. I was totally out of my depth, Sable, and I got scared and ran. I can't handle stuff like that. Look,' she temporised, 'I'm sorry—I really am. I owe you so much—you really saved me, and I'm really grateful to you—but I *can't* live the life you lead, Sable! Some can, some can't. That's it.'

'OK,' agreed Sable, 'I admit I like sex a lot—always have done! But listen, Ros, all you really need is *one* rich bloke! That's all. He'd get you out of this dump so fast you wouldn't see daylight.' She gave a sudden giggle. 'Well, you probably wouldn't see daylight anyway. If I were a bloke I'd lock you in my bedroom and never let you out! Oh, Ros.' She gave a frustrated wail. '*Why* don't you lighten up more? You could have such *fun*!'

It was a familiar argument, and one that could only end the same way it always did.

Rosalind looked away. 'I won't sleep my way out of debt, Sable—that's all there is to it.'

The other girl gave an exasperated sigh. 'You're wasting your youth, Ros! You're wasting it slaving away like a drudge. It's a time that will never come back—and you'll have nothing to show for it. Not even memories. Zilch.

Time's ticking on—God, thirty's on its way. Looks don't last for ever! I should know! And there's another bunch of younger girls treading on my heels already! I've got to score while I can.' Her voice changed, taking on an urgent note. 'That's why I've just *got* to get things sorted with Yuri! I've got to get him sweet on me again—I mean, really sweet. So…' She took a deep breath and looked Rosalind straight in the eyes. 'That's why I want you to come out with us tonight! It would sort of say sorry to him for walking out, you know.'

Rosalind's answer was an automatic reflex.

'No way!'

'Ros—'

'Sable, no. I can't. I'm sorry. I just don't want to go anywhere near Yuri Rostrov.' She paused minutely. She still didn't know if Sable knew that her boyfriend was a fully paid-up gangster, not some flash-cash businessman, and that therefore the very last thing on earth she intended doing was going anywhere near him again. She had a pretty grim feeling that Sable must know—but presumably she liked to keep to the sanitised version, and Rosalind didn't particularly want to explain how it was she had found out that Yuri Rostrov was *not* a legitimate businessman.

Tentatively, Rosalind began, 'Sable, look, I really do appreciate how much I owe you, but—'

The other girl cut across her. 'No. You don't.' There was something wary in the way Sable spoke. Rosalind frowned. Sable went on. 'You don't owe me. You owe Yuri.'

'*What?*'

Sable looked uncomfortable. 'The thing is, a few months ago I got a bit carried away when we were out gambling—I lost Yuri quite a lot of money. He wasn't too thrilled. I wasn't going to be able to pay him back any time soon, so I…well, I said I knew someone who owed me more than I owed him, and he said, OK, I could transfer the debt to him and pass him the repayments you make. Which is what I've been doing. So, technically speaking, it's him you owe the money to.'

'I owe seven thousand euros to Yuri Rostrov?' Rosalind's voice was a sick thread.

Sable gave a would-be nonchalant shrug. 'It isn't really such a big deal, Ros. You keep paying me the installments and Yuri's happy. Anyway, the reason I told you was to show you why it's a good idea for both of us to keep him sweet. That's why I want you to come along tonight. He'll get his precious face back, and then he'll stop sulking at me. Don't worry, I'll make sure you get to do a runner before the clock strikes midnight and you turn into fallen woman!'

There was a waspish note to her voice, but Rosalind wasn't listening. Her mind had blanked out—only one thought sat in it, occupying the total space in a terrifying, obliterating way.

She owed seven thousand euros to a gangster.

Dear God, wasn't it bad enough being thousands and thousands of euros in debt? Money it was taking her for ever to repay. But to find that she owed it to Yuri Rostrov…

In her head she heard Cesar Montarez's warning echo. *Men like Rostrov are dangerous—he won't blink an eyelid before having you killed…*

She wanted to give a hysterical laugh, but fought it down. She had to stay calm. She had to.

But she could feel the horror rising in her throat.

Sable was talking again. 'So, I'll come along here this evening, and I'll lend you that outfit again, and then we'll meet up with Yuri at his hotel and—'

'I can't.'

Rosalind's voice was sharp.

'What do you mean?'

'I can't. Not tonight.'

'Ros, the café can close early for once. I need you to help me out—I really do.'

But Rosalind was immune to the mix of pleading and impatience in Sable's voice. All she knew was that the last, the very last thing on earth she could do was go anywhere near a man who was a ruthless, murderous gangster with a taste for naked hot-tubbing in his suite, whose grotesque side-kick had been all over her and to whom she owed seven thousand crippling, terrifying euros…

'I can't,' she said again. 'You see…' Her brain floundered wildly, desperately trying to think of a reason to put Sable off. And where the words came from she simply didn't know, but they did all the same. 'You see, I've got a date tonight.'

CHAPTER THREE

ROSALIND could feel the nervous tension in her stomach as she got out of the taxi and walked up to the huge pillared front of the Casino El Paraíso.

Was she mad to be here?

It had been impulse—sheer, terrified impulse—that had made her blurt out to Sable that she couldn't meet up with Yuri Rostrov and company that night because she had a date. Sable had immediately wanted to know more—clearly thinking she was just stringing her a line—and with huge reluctance Rosalind had told her that it was someone she had encountered at El Paraíso who had made a play for her.

Sable's eyes had widened. 'Rich?'

Rosalind had nodded reluctantly.

'That's great! Ros, this could be it for you!' Sable's voice had sounded genuinely pleased for her. 'Listen, this makes everything different! You go off tonight with this guy of yours. I'll tell Yuri there's a good chance you'll be able to get the money you owe him really soon—he'll like that. He'll understand that you can't afford to stand this guy of yours up. And you mustn't, Ros! Rich guys like you to be all over them. Take it from me—I know—I'm an expert! Speaking of which, if you want any tips on how to make it really hot in the sack for him, come to me—I've got a repertoire that would make your hair curl! But save it for when you really need it, you know? If you see signs of him going off you.'

Her eyes had gleamed. 'I am dead, dead curious about this guy—he just *has* to be something if he's actually managed to get you to go out with him! Jeez, I *knew* you just needed to get a sniff at the high life to make you want to chuck in this drop-dead drudgery you insist on! Play your cards right, Ros, and you can kiss it goodbye for ever! And listen, Ros,' she'd urged, 'you've got to play it really, really carefully when it comes to the money! Get him well and truly hooked first, then go for it! You don't want to make it too obvious it's the money you're after—these guys like to think you'd be with them even if they were dirt-poor—they're all dead vain about themselves and their sexual prowess! Even when they're totally useless at it. But at the same time—' a serious note had entered her voice '—it would be really smart to get some dosh off him as soon as you can. If I can hand over a big wodge from you to Yuri, that would really help—do us both good! And you won't have to worry about Yuri after tonight anyway—he wants to go to Monte Carlo for a while, so that will leave the coast clear for you with this bloke!'

She'd given Rosalind a huge grin and a double thumbs-up sign. 'Anyway, I am really, really thrilled for you that you've wised up and pulled at last! You go for it, girl! High life, here you come! You are going to have *such* a fun time from now on!'

Rosalind hadn't answered. She'd hardly been listening to Sable. She'd been thinking instead that she must have been mad to say she had a date with Cesar Montarez!

Would he even want to see her? Since dropping her off he hadn't exactly come chasing after her the next day, had he? Maybe he'd totally forgotten all about her?

And now it was her chasing after him.

She felt herself flush with embarrassment at what she was proposing to do: present herself to a man who owned a string of fancy resorts just because he'd expressed a passing fancy for her—a man whose image had been haunting her ever since she'd set eyes on him!—and hope he'd let her stick around his casino for the evening to give her the alibi she needed to keep her away from Yuri Rostrov in the one place where she knew he wouldn't be given house-room.

Her spine chilled at the thought of the gangster. Embarrassment was the least of her problems.

But as she approached the double doors of the casino it looked as if she was about to hit yet another problem. The grand-looking doorman stepped forward.

'Excuse me, *señorita*, you are with...?'

He spoke very politely, but his bulk was in front of the door—which he was not opening for her.

Rosalind paused.

'I'm not with anyone—' she began.

The doorman bowed his head again. 'In which case, *señorita*, I regret that you may not go in.'

Rosalind stared at him. 'I'm over twenty-one,' she said. Could the man *really* think she was underage or something?

The man shook his head slightly.

'I regret, *señorita*, that it is house policy not to admit unaccompanied ladies.'

The penny dropped. Rosalind felt her face first flushing, then draining.

She looked totally different tonight from the way she'd looked wearing Sable's trashy number, and she had hoped that would make her acceptable. Tonight she looked far more like the kind of female who would frequent such an upmarket place. The dress she was wearing was the single one left over from the days when she had splashed money around like there was no tomorrow. Well, tomorrow had arrived, all right, and it was here right now—with a vengeance she hadn't dreamed of. Yet the chiffon whisper of the gossamer material as it shushed around her legs whisked her instantly back to those happier times, so long ago now, when she'd swanned around the beautiful places of the Spanish *costa* as if she'd had every right to be there.

Memory stabbed at her, but she put it aside. There was no time for painful memories now.

'I...I was here the other evening,' she faltered, hoping that might work.

The man was unmoved. 'I regret, *señorita*,' was all he said. His eyes glanced beyond her, to some waiting taxis clearly on hold for any patrons who might require them, and he nodded at a driver. The taxi began to glide forward.

'May I, *señorita*?' The doorman indicated the approaching taxi.

Rosalind stared, appalled. *No! I can't be thrown out before I've even got in! I can't!*

'Just a moment!' Rapidly she clicked open her handbag and drew out a slip of card. 'Señor Montarez asked me to come!' she said quickly, and handed the business card to the doorman. 'He gave me this the other night!'

Expressionlessly the man took it, and just as expressionlessly took in the fact that, yes, indeed, this extremely lovely but unaccompanied female was telling the truth. He handed the card back to Rosalind.

'One moment, if you please. Your name, *señorita*?'

Rosalind told him, her fingers crossing desperately in the folds of her skirt.

The doorman took out a mobile phone, keyed in a number, and after a brief moment spoke.

'Señorita Foster is here, Señor Montarez.' His voice sounded a little diffident, but that was all. A moment later he had disconnected. 'Please enter, Señorita Foster,' said the doorman, and ushered her through into the casino.

Weak with relief, she hurried inside. There was the huge lobby, with its acre of carpet and a wide set of shallow stairs to one side. She had hardly gazed around her when someone came lithely down the staircase, slipping a mobile phone inside his jacket pocket.

Her breath caught. Just as it had the first time she'd set eyes on Cesar Montarez.

And the second time.

And now the third.

He walked up to her, as fabulous now as he had been

before, looking a million dollars in his superbly cut tuxedo, lean and tall—and oh, so beautiful...

He stopped in front of her. She felt faint. His dark, beautiful eyes looked down at her, rich with pleasure.

'You came.'

It was all he said. All he needed to say.

All her reasons for coming here, all her dread about Yuri Rostrov, owing seven thousand euros to a gangster, simply evaporated.

Instead, she stared up at Cesar Montarez, who had not turned her away, who had not frowned and tried to think who she was, who had not been annoyed at her presenting herself on his doorstep—who had walked right up to her and looked at her as if she were the most welcome sight in the world.

'Yes,' she answered him. It was all she needed to say.

He took her hands and raised them, one by one, to his mouth. His eyes were dark, oh, so dark, and the expression in them... Oh, it just melted her to little pieces...

'Come,' said Cesar Montarez, and tucked her hand into his arm, and led her off.

Triumph soared through Cesar. Triumph, and deep, deep satisfaction. He'd been right all along. Despite the fact that it had taken her two nights to show up. Nights spent absolutely convinced that at any moment, any moment, he would glimpse her among the guests and would move forward and claim her. If she hadn't shown up tonight he'd have gone after her, no question.

And now she was here. The satisfaction surged again. And the anticipation. Oh yes, definitely the anticipation.

So she had been playing hard to get. That was fine by him. It had merely whetted his appetite, that was all. She'd kept him waiting, and that was fine by him, too. It had merely increased the edge of his hunger.

And that would only increase the pleasure of the feasting.

As she walked beside him across the lobby and into one of the many bar areas the scent of her skin caught at him. She was wearing no perfume but her own. As for her gown—oh, it was as if he had never seen her in that trashy lamé tart-skin the other evening. Tonight she had dressed as a woman of her beauty ought to dress! With a restraint that only threw her loveliness into greater relief. The plain black, so elegantly cut, sleeveless, like a shift, with a high neckline, her burnished hair drawn back into a low chignon, drew total attention to her face. And this time her face was worth every tribute. Tonight, her make-up was dramatic, but not overdone. Her eyes were deep and shadowed, but her skin was uncovered, the fineness of her English complexion, only lightly tanned, needing no foundation or powder. And her mouth was glossed, that was all—a mouth prepared for kissing…

But not yet. The night was young. He would savour it. Savour the pleasure of letting her beauty enthral him, entice him. Hold back from her to increase both his appetite and hers, while knowing, with deep, pleasurable certainty, that there would be no restraint by the end of the evening, that the consummation of the pulsing desire he was already feeling would receive full and total satiation.

But to reach such a consummation certain rituals must first be observed.

He led her towards the long curving bar, and paused to smile down at her.

'Champagne?' he asked.

Rosalind nodded dumbly. She was probably incapable of speech, she thought. Her heart was skittering in her chest, her lips parted and breathless.

She had eyes only for him.

Cesar Montarez.

Who was smiling down at her and making her heart go skittering away.

His eyes glanced away from her to the attentively waiting barman, and she felt it as a loss she could not bear.

What's happening to me? Why am I feeling like this?

But she didn't want to answer. Didn't want to think. Wanted only for Cesar Montarez to look at her again—and to gaze at that devastating face, and drink it in until she was intoxicated by the sight of it.

In a daze she heard the soft pop of a champagne cork, and realised that she was being handed a beading, gently fizzing flute of golden wine.

'Thank you for coming tonight.'

His voice was warm, like a caress. She went on gazing at him as his eyes bathed her in his regard.

He touched his glass to hers.

'To the evening ahead,' he murmured.

She could not answer, could not say a word. She seemed bereft of sense, as well as speech. Instead, she wordlessly sipped at her champagne, feeling the bubbles tingle through her, slipping into her bloodstream.

He smiled down at her, his gaze washing over her with a lingering appreciation that set her blood racing.

'You are exquisite,' he told her. 'So very beautiful.'

His eyes told her so, as well as his words.

'So are you,' she answered, the words coming before she could stop them.

A smile quirked at his mouth, as though her answer had both amused and pleased him. He bent his head a fraction lower. She felt even fainter.

'Then I foresee a wonderful evening ahead of us,' he said, and the smile was in his voice, in his eyes. And more than a smile—oh, much, much more.

She had become another person. Of that she was certain. The other Rosalind, who had existed up until the moment when Cesar Montarez had walked towards her and taken her hand in his, had simply ceased to exist. Oh, she was out there somewhere, in the shadows, but Rosalind could not see her any more, could not feel her. Could not feel her fear and dread, could not feel her revulsion at the mess she had got herself into with a bunch of gangsters...

Cesar Montarez simply blotted her out of existence, that other Rosalind.

And called this Rosalind into existence—wonderful, magical existence!

She drifted at his side, feeling as light as air, floating on a cloud of bliss, feeling the dark promise of his presence at her side, supremely conscious of his lean, potent strength, the wash of his dark eyes on her, the play of his sculpted lips, the heady scent of his maleness, intoxicating her like liquor!

'So,' he murmured as they left the bar area, 'you came at last. Why did you keep me waiting so long?'

His eyes were warm on her face, like a caress. She could not answer. He smiled, and softly brushed her cheek with the back of his fingers. She let the bliss of the sensation wash through her.

'No matter.' He smiled again. 'You are here—that is all that is important.'

Yes, she thought dreamily, floating on a haze of happiness. That is all that is important. Nothing else is—

Certainly nothing as sordid, as scary, as owing seven thousand euros to a gangster...

'Tell me.' His voice tightened suddenly. 'You have told your friend you will be doing no more favours for her? I don't have to warn you, do I, not to go near Yuri Rostrov again?'

She shook her head sharply. 'No! No, I don't want anything more to do with him!' There was a fervour about her answer that satisfied him.

'That is as well,' he said soberly. 'He is not a man to get involved with, however remotely. Stay away from him—and from anyone who knows him.'

A flicker of fear had shown in her eyes briefly. Again, it satisfied him. Naïve she might be, but he had to get the message across to her—the likes of Yuri Rostrov were far too dangerous for her. And far too sordid.

Rosalind saw the stiffening of revulsion in his eyes, and felt guilt pinch at her.

The other Rosalind came crowding back.

Tell him! came a voice from deep inside. Tell him why you are really here! Tell him that you are running scared of Yuri Rostrov, that you came here tonight simply because it was the one place you knew he wouldn't be, and because it gave you an excuse to avoid him. Tell him you're up to your neck in debt to him!

But she couldn't tell him. The words wouldn't come. She didn't want them to. She didn't want to see Cesar Montarez's revulsion at Yuri Rostrov become revulsion at her as well. She couldn't bear it.

Tonight was a dream—a brief, blissful dream in which she was wafting around on the arm of the most gorgeous man in the world, who smiled down at her with dark, desiring eyes. She couldn't destroy that dream.

And what would be the point? She was only here for the evening. Oh, Sable might think that she was here to take herself a rich lover and get herself out of debt, but Rosalind knew better. That way was not for her—it was quite impossible to contemplate behaving in such a way! No, this was just one magical Cinderella night for her. One short evening while she stayed out of Yuri Rostrov's way and let herself bask in the bliss that was Cesar Montarez's company. And he seemed to want nothing but hers in return.

She slipped willingly back into the dream that was Cesar Montarez. Hers for one brief evening—before reality returned with cold, sickening vengeance.

But not quite yet.

He took her to the roulette tables, where a chair magically appeared for her, and as she took her place, her gossamer skirts pooling gracefully around her, he stood behind her, his hand pressing on the chair-back. She could feel him— feel the warmth, the strength of his body—and her blood raced. She dipped her head, sipping from her champagne.

He leant forward, pushing a handful of chips towards her.

'Choose a number,' he invited.

She gave one at random, and watched him make the play, looking with all the other players at the wheel spinning, and slowing, and coming to a halt at quite another number. For a moment she felt dismay, and then realised with a sense of light-headedness that since he owned the whole casino the loss could hardly count!

The croupier called another play, and she took another chip, entering into the spirit of things. This time she picked her birthday, only to see it lose again. She twisted her head back.

'You choose!' She laughed.

His eyes gleamed and he reached forward, pushing a pile of chips onto yet another numbered square. Again, for a brief moment Rosalind felt a qualm, but stilled it. How could Cesar Montarez lose against himself? Or win? The whole thing was nothing more than an amusing exercise.

As the wheel slowed she felt her breath catch. The ball continued to roll around until, with widening eyes, Rosalind watched it nestle into a particular slot—the very number that her chips were on—and hold!

She gasped, clapping her hands with pleasure, and heard Cesar laugh as well.

'My turn again!' she exclaimed, and placed a fresh piece on yet another number. This time she won, and she clapped her hands again, and toasted Cesar in champagne.

From then on her luck came and went—mostly went. At last there were only a few chips left in front of her, and she made a face, getting to her feet.

'Time to quit while I'm ahead,' she said ruefully.

Cesar's mouth quirked. 'Sensible girl. Come—'

He held his hand out to her and she took it, and moved away with him.

The dream was still floating her away—she couldn't resist it. It was lifting all the weights and worries of her life, leaving them far, far below.

And she wouldn't, couldn't spoil the dream—the only time she would ever have with him.

Because that was what Cesar Montarez was; she knew in her heart of hearts. Nothing more than a dream. He was like some wonderful fantasy, like watching a film where the most fabulous film star in the world suddenly reached out through the screen and drew her up into the glamorous un-reality of his world.

Tomorrow she would have to face up to the hideous mess she was in.

But not now.

Not yet.

'Rosalind?'

His accented voice cut through her anguished mental ag-itation. For a moment her mind went completely blank, and then, recovering herself, she heard herself saying, 'Is there a seaview from the casino terrace?'

She watched his mouth quirk. 'A very beautiful view—would you like to see it?'

He guided her towards the arching French windows that opened in a parade to the wide cantilevered terrace beyond. The view was indeed fantastic. Rosalind wafted forward, resting her hands on the stone balcony, gazing out. The land sloped away, cunningly landscaped so that the hotel and its little private villas were hardly visible through the artfully placed trees and greenery. Only the marina down by the sea's edge was highlighted, the expensive yachts swinging slowly at their moorings. The night air was sweet, rich with the sound of cicadas, the stars blazing in the heavens. Far out to sea on the surface of the water the starlight gleamed and was gone.

She gazed around, drinking in the view, feeling the soft night air play in her hair, on her bare arms.

Then, as she gazed, she felt another touch to her skin.

She stood quite still as Cesar Montarez moved behind her, the tips of his fingers lightly, oh, so lightly grazing up and down her upper arms.

Almost she leaned into him, wanting to feel the length of his body behind her, wanting to feel his hands close over her arms, drawing her back against him.

But she held still. To move, to move at all, would be to invite him. To respond to him with a blatant invitation—yes, would he please seduce her? Would he please caress her, kiss her, take her to his bed...?

And she could not be that blatant—could not.

So she simply went on standing there, while time slowed right down. The entire universe focused in so that there was nothing left in it, nothing at all except the feel of his fingertips slowly, so slowly, drifting up and down her skin...

Every muscle in her body was tense. The effort of holding herself still was quite excruciating, yet she could not move—could not even break away. She could only go on standing there, immobile, her breath coming low and silent, her eyes shuttering as she felt the slow bliss of his drifting touch.

'Cesar! There you are!'

The loud voice hailing him was brutal in its interruption. Rosalind started, and immediately Cesar's hands abandoned her. She felt him move slightly, and turn away from her.

'Pat—it's good to see you.'

His voice was bland, urbane. Rosalind used the moment to take a deep breath and turn her body to see what was happening.

A man had come up to Cesar, late middle-aged, in a white dinner jacket, with a glass of whisky in his hand.

'Now, have you given any more thought to what I said

the other day, Cesar?' the man enquired, his Irish accent audible.

'Of course,' Cesar answered smoothly. It looked good on paper, the business proposition that Pat O'Hanran was promoting—a new deluxe golf club that would combine the O'Hanran brand name with the El Paraíso track record in luxury resorts. Nevertheless, after a few moments of business discussion about the prospect of a mutually advantageous joint venture, he succeeded in halting the other man.

'If it's convenient I'll come along tomorrow with my architect and landscape designer and look at the practicalities of the site you propose,' he suggested.

The notion found favour, and with a wry glance at Rosalind the Irishman finished the conversation and headed back indoors.

'My apologies,' murmured Cesar.

'Please—I don't mean to monopolise you,' Rosalind returned diffidently.

The dark eyes gleamed.

'You do more than that,' he told her, his voice low and husky. He took her arm. 'But, tell me, what would you like to do next? Try your luck at the tables again? Some more champagne? Would you like to dine now? Or...' the gleam came again, and made her feel suddenly hot '...perhaps you would like to admire the view from here a little longer?'

'Food sounds great!' replied Rosalind, her voice suddenly croaky.

His mouth quirked. 'Of course,' he said smoothly.

Too smoothly.

What am I doing? thought Rosalind, as she sat opposite Cesar Montarez in the windowed bay of the casino's restaurant. It was crowded, but whether it was the artful spacing of the tables, or simply that no one else in the room seemed to exist any more, she felt as though he was the only person there.

The food was superb. Meltingly she savoured the delicate seafood terrine, sipping at her chilled white wine. It had been an age since she had eaten like this, and for a moment memory tugged at her with poignant anguish. Then she put it aside. That time was gone—and this time, now, was going to be all too fleeting. Don't spoil it with memories, she told herself. And don't spoil it by thinking about reality. Tonight will be over soon enough, and tomorrow will have to be dealt with—but not yet.

Not yet.

What they talked about as they ate she had no recollection. Nothing difficult, nothing demanding. She asked him about El Paraíso and found herself fascinated by how a luxury resort was set up and operated. Seamlessly he moved on to talk about the other El Paraíso resorts, and then about the conditions of tourism and development in Spain itself.

'It is both a blessing and a curse,' he told her. 'Offering much, but taking much away as well.'

'It's certainly a blessing for Brits who can't stand the British winter!' she observed.

'You've been here some time, you said?'

She nodded. 'Yes, nearly three years now.'

'What brought you here? A holiday and then you decided to stay?'

She smiled uncertainly. 'Sort of. I…came with some-one…and then stayed on.'

'And your…companion?'

She glanced away. 'I'm on my own now,' she answered, and her eyes slid back to his of their own accord.

The slightest smile of satisfaction played around his mouth.

She found it hard to look away again.

Dinner was a long, lingering affair. Once or twice Rosalind got the impression that people were trying to catch Cesar's eye—either guests or, she assumed, some of his employees.

But, apart from casual greetings to some of the guests who approached him personally, he made no attempt to divert his attention from her.

Even when one of those seeking his attention was a svelte, breathtaking blonde.

She was clearly with another man, Rosalind could see, on the other side of the room. But at the end of their meal, as her escort was busying himself with signing the chit, the woman rose to her feet and made her way with gliding purpose towards Cesar Montarez.

'Cesar—'

Her voice was breathy, with a distinct Nordic accent. She was wearing what was obviously an extremely expensive ice-blue number from a well-known Milanese fashion house, low-cut and very clinging. A showy diamond necklace and earrings glittered on her tanned skin. Quite unselfconsciously the woman bent, bestowing a lingering kiss on Cesar's cheek.

'It's been too long…' The breathy voice came again. 'Ilsa.'

Cesar's voice was restrained. Rosalind would have had to have been deaf not to hear that note in it. So would the other woman—but, whether or not she heard it, she ignored it.

'We should get together now that I'm back in Spain. Take the yacht out. Find a little privacy.' Her smile lingered, like the look she gave him. 'The way we used to.'

'I'm a little preoccupied these days, Ilsa.'

Cesar's voice was courteous, but Rosalind could hear the steel beneath it.

A pair of ice-blue eyes, a perfect match for her dress, darted in her direction—and dismissed her.

'Well, Cesar, *querida*.' The woman's crimson-tipped fingernails rested briefly on his shoulder. 'When you've finished with your little…preoccupation…' the dismissive glance came Rosalind's way again '...let me know. If I'm still around...'

The woman lifted her hand from Cesar's shoulder and glanced at Rosalind again.

'Enjoy tonight. It's probably all you'll get.'

She glided away again, her poison darting home.

There was a moment's silence. Then Cesar spoke.

'My apologies.'

Rosalind gave a slight shake of her head.

'De nada.' The Spanish phrase rolled off her tongue.

She meant it, too. After all, the information that ice-blue Ilsa had given had hardly been telling her something she hadn't known all along.

But you're not going to stay the night, anyway.

No, of course she wasn't. That would be insane. Cesar Montarez might be the most breathtaking male she'd ever seen, but he was little more than a stranger.

He wouldn't be by morning... whispered that voice inside her head again, offering her things she knew she must not take.

But she couldn't leave—not quite yet. It was all right to stay a little longer, linger over her liqueur, let her mouth speak inconsequential words while her eyes simply drank in the beauty of Cesar Montarez.

That smile was playing over his mouth again. He'd done it off and on all through the meal, as though he were contemplating something.

'You are very forbearing,' he remarked. 'It is generous of you. Ilsa Tronberg is a very spoilt woman. She caught a rich, elderly husband, divorced him, and is now cruising the Mediterranean enjoying her settlement—the yacht was thrown in for free!—while she decides which wealthy man is going to have the privilege of keeping her while she banks the remainder.'

His voice sounded cynical. Rosalind wasn't surprised. But then she could hardly be surprised that a rich, beautiful divorcee like the ice-blue blonde would like to put her ring on Cesar Montarez's finger—most rich men were nothing in the gorgeousness stakes. Cesar Montarez, rich *and* gorgeous, would be a prize for any spoilt, ambitious woman.

A prize for any woman.

She shook her head mentally. That wasn't a pleasant way to think about him. OK, so his wealth lent him buckets of glamour—she'd be a total hypocrite to deny that!—but it wasn't his wealth that was keeping her here, sitting opposite him, drinking him in like vintage champagne.

For the first time in her life she felt profoundly a deep gratitude that she had been blessed with beauty herself. Because she knew that had she not been so blessed then she would not have been sitting here. That Cesar Montarez would not even know she existed.

And he certainly would not be smiling at her through those half-shuttered eyes, while that smile played around his mouth and made her want to reach her fingers forward and press them to his lips, as if she could catch his smile with her fingertips.

'Poor woman,' she heard herself say.

The smile stilled. *'Que?'*

'She can hardly be happy, living like that.' Rosalind's voice was openly pitying.

Cesar was looking at her as if he didn't quite believe what she was saying.

'Most women envy her,' he replied dryly. 'She is fantastic-looking, well-off, and still young. The world is at her feet.'

Rosalind wondered for a moment whether to say what she really thought—that that might all be true, but what kind of life must it be 'cruising the Mediterranean' on the lookout for another rich man to marry…?

But then, with a pang, she realised that for a man like Cesar Montarez, and for those who moved in his circles, the hunt for riches was endless, however they were gained.

Hadn't he just told her over dinner how he'd started with nothing but a loan from the bank and built his resort empire from scratch in twelve years? Of course wealth was important to him—it would be absurd to say otherwise.

And the last thing she wanted to do now was spoil this magical evening out of time by starting a heavy-duty discussion about what made for happiness and whether that had to include shedloads of money.

So, instead, she simply gave him a baiting smile.

'But not you. You're not at her feet, it seems,' she commented dryly.

Their eyes met, and Rosalind's heart gave a little skip.

'I never was, believe me.'

No, thought Rosalind, you simply slept with her, that's all.

It was a sobering reminder—or it should have been. The trouble was, even as the words formed in her mind, so did an image to go with them. Oh, not of ice-blue Ilsa, slowly peeling off that clinging evening gown while Cesar Montarez watched her with waiting eyes, but of herself performing that office. She saw herself slide the zip on her dress, let the material fall from her shoulders, slipping from her body while all the while Cesar stood, watching her, his entire being focused on her...waiting to take her to his bed....

CHAPTER FOUR

SHE felt a flush go through her body, warm and dilating.

'What are you thinking about?'

He did not need to ask, not even in that amused, oh-so-intimate tone. He already knew the answer. Had known it from the moment he'd seen the daze in her eyes, watched the blood flush visibly across her creamy skin.

He felt himself respond to it, felt the swift surge of quickening. It had been coming and going all evening, and he had had to fight increasingly hard not to let it overpower him. The battle itself had been enjoyable, testing his own strength in resisting a growing need simply to cut to the chase, to take this beautiful, enticing woman off to his private quarters where he could be finally completely undisturbed with her. And because he knew that that was exactly what would happen by the end of the evening he could take pleasure now in reining in his own desire. For it meant that the moment when he could at last let go of that fine control and indulge his every desire for her would be all the sweeter for it.

Certainly, apart from Pat O'Hanran—who had, to do him justice, beaten a retreat pretty promptly when he'd realised he was *de trop*—and Ilsa Tronberg—clearly on the prowl for him again—he'd been given a wide berth this evening. His staff had got the message loud and clear, and it had taken nothing more than a quelling glance to dispose of any of them who had thought they could catch him for a quick word about matters which, right now, were of little concern to him. He hired the best, paid them handsomely, and they didn't need babysitting.

Not tonight.

Tonight he had other matters on his agenda.

Such as enjoying the way that Rosalind Foster was trying to pretend that she wasn't thinking, right now, of the pleasures to come…

Her stumbling, 'Oh, nothing!' in answer to his query merely amused him. She'd been thinking of him, and what would be happening with him very soon, that was certain— he knew when a woman was becoming aroused, and Rosalind Foster was showing all the signs. The flush, the dilating eyes, the feathering looks, the pulse at her slender throat, the fluttering of her hands…

The smile played around his mouth again. She would be good, he knew. Very good indeed.

Like a restless stallion beneath a master rider, his desire kicked again, letting its presence be felt.

Soon, he told it. *But not quite yet…*

'Tell me,' he said, his voice little more than conversational again, 'what have you seen of Spain since you were here? Or do you simply prefer to stay by the coast?'

Grateful for a return to ordinary topics that did not refer to Cesar Montarez's former sexual partners—let alone his anticipated immediate future one!—Rosalind took up the question.

'Oh, I've managed to do the obvious tourist things—the Alhambra, Granada, Seville, Jerez. We never got very far north, however, so I've never seen Madrid and Estremadura, or the north coast or the Pyrenees. I'd have liked to have seen some of the battlefield sites from the Peninsular War but—' She broke off. 'Well, perhaps another time.'

If he noticed her hesitation he made no comment. Instead, he said, the note of surprise not completely concealed, 'Battlefield sites?'

'Yes—Badajoz, Ciudad Rodrigo, Salamanca—all those places. I suppose it's a bit morbid,' she allowed, 'but the names are so evocative. Even though, of course, they were such terrible times for Spain.'

Cesar was looking at her curiously. 'Have you been a student of history—you seem very knowledgeable?'

She shook her head straight away. She'd never studied anything interesting—just useful. Like the secretarial and business studies course she'd taken to enable her to get work locally and go on living at home, bringing in an extra wage. Her eyes shadowed. That was all gone now, and instead here she was, being wined and dined in five-star luxury by a five-star man. She wanted to keep her real life as far away from this magical evening as she could.

So all she answered to his question was, 'I've always loved historical novels, especially from that period, and the Peninsular War is such an obviously exciting setting for them.' She gave a self-mocking smile. 'Like most women I'm a sucker for the uniforms from that era! All the men, of whatever nationality, were so dashing and glamorous! Yes, I know that in reality it was terrible and bloodthirsty, and so many men—and women—died, and there were such atrocities by the French, and the Spanish in retaliation, but even so…' She shrugged. 'There's just something about that period that fascinates me!'

Cesar leant back in his chair and gave a laugh. He looked relaxed suddenly, and twice as sexy, Rosalind registered.

'I should be stern and tell you that war is not glamorous or fascinating at all—*por Dios*, is Spain not still haunted by the memories of our own hideous Civil War that tore us apart, with wounds still not yet healed?—and yet…' His eyes danced. 'I have to confess that when I was a student I, too, chose the Napoleonic era to specialise in. And I confess, too, to sometimes wishing that for perhaps a week or two, no more, I could try out being someone like Don Julian Sanchez, a fierce, bold guerrilla who mercilessly harried the French during the War of Independence. He and his like were very wild, virtually brigands. They were used by the regular forces for reconnaissance and intelligence gathering, and one of the most remarkable things Don Julian did was to capture the French governor of Ciudad Rodrigo when he was out hunting, and hand him over to Wellington as a prize. I believe the governor thought himself fortunate he wasn't skewered on the spot!'

For a moment the image of Cesar Montarez accoutred as a wild, hard-riding, hard-fighting guerrilla captivated Rosalind. Then she shook her head.

'No—it sounds far too rough for you! I can far more easily see you in Moorish clothes—those beautiful flowing robes...'

He gave another laugh and leant forward. 'I can see you have an active imagination, *querida*. I foresee some... interesting...episodes between us. I am sure it would not be too difficult for me to find such robes, if it would...please you...'

His eyes were dancing still, but the expression in them was more than amused. Rosalind felt the flush spreading out through her skin, and looked hastily down at her liqueur glass. He reached out a hand, gently drawing one finger down the line of her cheek and tipping it under her chin to lift it before letting her go.

'You make me feel like a Moor,' he said softly. 'Such downcast eyes, such hesitance—such promise...'

She swallowed, her throat tight. Her breath seemed too tight for her body.

I've got to go! This is getting out of hand!

The impulse formed in her panic. She must go—she really must! Her resistance was weakening with every moment that she stayed in Cesar Montarez's company.

Then, in his normal conversational voice again, he went on, 'Do you know, I don't believe I have ever discussed the Peninsular War with a woman before? At least not one under fifty! I had one very excellent university professor, however, who was female—she was an expert on the Reconquista. Perhaps she had been inspired by that most indomitable queen, Isabella of Castile!'

Rosalind looked at him. 'Did you really study history?' she asked. 'I would have thought something like economics or accountancy would have been your subject.'

He gave his quirking smile again, and a touch of self-mockery showed in his eyes.

'When I was young I considered money tedious, like so many of the young do. I have since discovered its advantages.'

His eyes glinted around the luxurious dining room that was just a fragment of his resort portfolio. There was satisfaction in his voice, as well as a pride that she guessed he deserved, having built it all from scratch.

She made her voice as neutral as she could, but it was hard. She had no quarrel with a man who could make a fortune—if he made it honestly, through hard work—and after all she was here enjoying the fruits of it for the evening—yet the contrast between what Cesar Montarez possessed and what she possessed—or rather did not possess—could hardly have been greater! The meal they had just eaten, not to mention the wines and the champagne, if he had been paying for it as a customer, would have come to well over a hundred euros alone!

She suppressed a sigh. There was no point thinking about it.

She could only enjoy this brief, magical respite from it.

Which was so nearly coming to an end.

But not quite yet.

'Do you prefer coffee? Or perhaps a very English cup of tea?' Cesar's query, the last three words said in an exaggeratedly English accent, brought a smile to her lips and came as a welcome delay. Yes, the evening was drawing to a close. The magic was nearly all spent.

But she would make the very most of the last of it.

'Coffee would be lovely,' she answered, following through by glancing around to see if there was a waiter cruising nearby. But to her consternation, as her gaze came back, she realised that Cesar was getting to his feet.

'The night is far too beautiful for us to waste it indoors,' he murmured, and came to help her up.

'Oh—where—?'

'I will show you. Come.'

She followed him meekly. Presumably there was another terrace somewhere, where guests could enjoy the fresh air along with their beverages. The bar had had such a terrace, now that she thought about it. But instead of heading towards the bar Cesar was taking her towards a bank of lifts.

'Um…' said Rosalind, hesitating automatically.

He glanced down at her again with that quirking smile.

'There is a higher terrace,' he told her. 'The views are even better than from the main terrace.'

'Um…' she said again, feeling jittery.

Just say you have to go now! Just say, Thank you very much but I have to go now. It's been a lovely evening. Goodbye.

She heard the words in her head. Felt her brain give the order for the words, give the order for her legs to stop walking towards the lift door which was opening now.

She walked right in, the words dying unsaid.

The doors of the lift sliced shut.

Instantly it was as if they were in the smallest space imaginable. As they were lifted away Rosalind felt her stomach stay behind. That was just the lift, wasn't it?

A second later they had come to a halt and the doors were whooshing open again. Rosalind hurried out. That chamber had just felt far, far too small.

She stopped dead.

She was in an apartment.

There was a little lobby, and then a reception room opening out beyond. Beautifully styled, spacious, elegant, softly lit—and deserted. On the far side were sliding doors opening to a riot of greenery.

Cesar ushered her forward.

'Um...' said Rosalind for the third time.

'Come,' said Cesar.

Her reluctance amused him. Shortly, he expected, she would say something about it being time for her to go. She'd drink her coffee first, and then smile politely and make a move.

So would he.

He opened the sliding doors and they slid noiselessly back, letting in the warmth of the air outside. Patio furniture was placed on the tiled floor, but Rosalind paid it no attention. Instead she was gazing out at the views. They were indeed even better than those from the main terrace. This apartment terrace was angled differently from the main casino terrace, so that more of the marina was shielded by the treetops, making the atmosphere darker, more private. The cicadas were going crazy up here, too, sounding louder and closer. Bougainvillaea rioted over the railings of the patio, and the heady scents of night flowers winnowed in the air. No noise filtered up from the casino below.

'It's beautiful!' she breathed.

'Yes,' said Cesar simply. It was indeed beautiful, and his architect had excelled himself in creating an apartment that was so convenient for the casino and yet so very private from it.

There was the sound of lift doors opening again, and Rosalind turned. One of the waiters from the restaurant was approaching them, bearing a tray of coffee.

'Jaime—*gracias.*'

Cesar nodded, and the young man came and set out the tray on the patio table. Then, with a murmur to his boss, he took his leave.

'Come and sit down.'

She might as well, Rosalind thought. After all that champagne and then the wine—white and red—and the liqueur, she could do with clearing her head a little. The coffee, hot and strong, was reviving, and she sipped it gratefully.

Cesar sat across from her, one ankle resting on his knee, his long, powerful thighs half widened. He leaned back in his padded chair, taking his coffee, obviously at his ease.

He looked incredible. The very image of a fantasy Latin lover.

Rosalind dropped her eyes, sipping again at her coffee and tucking her feet back.

They talked lazily. Cesar remained relaxed, and although Rosalind found it disturbing to look him in the eyes too long, he was a good few feet away from her, and posed no immediate threat. He laughed more here, his white teeth gleaming, making him look younger. At one point he set his empty cup down, and before refilling it—and hers—cricked his neck and undid his bow tie, slipping open the top button of his dress shirt.

He sat back.

Rosalind stared, unable to tear her eyes away.

God, but there was something about a man in evening dress with a loose tie and an open collar! Something that simply went *Thunk!* all the way through her. He still looked svelte, and elegant, and oh-so-expensive, but the slight token of undress, however little it was actually revealing, simply sent shivers through her. He looked, the word came to her, raffish.

And very, very sexy.

She took her refilled cup numbly.

Oh, my girl, it is time to go—with bells on!

But she couldn't. Not yet. Not quite yet. She still had a cup of coffee to finish. And besides, Cesar was talking about a visit he'd made a while ago to the Canaries, and taking a boat out and watching dolphins...

Rosalind sat, sipping her coffee, and drank it up. Drank him up.

Her cup was empty. Regretfully, she set it down. There was no clock to strike midnight, but it had struck all the same. She had to go. The evening was over—she couldn't eke it out any longer.

She stood up.

Immediately Cesar did likewise.

'I have to go,' said Rosalind.

He came towards her.

'Why?' he asked, stopping in front of her. There was nothing more in his voice than mild enquiry, yet Rosalind's breath felt tight.

'Because,' she answered.

'Because you don't do one-night stands—is that it?'

Hearing the ugly English phrase echoed back at her made her flinch. Then she shrugged. It was the truth, however ugly the phrase.

'Yes.'

He gave a little shake of his head. 'This will not be what you insist on calling a one-night stand. Why do you make things ugly—' his voice was low '—when they are so...beautiful? As beautiful as you, Rosalind *querida*.'

As his voice softened he reached out a hand, touching her chignon, his thumb just grazing the nape of her neck below.

She felt her skin quiver.

He did nothing more, just stood there, his thumb slowly moving across her nape, so lightly.

'You are very beautiful, Rosalind. And tonight will be

beautiful, too. You will not call it by an ugly name that has no truth it in. Tonight is made for desire, and there is desire between us. If you deny that you lie, and you will not do that, will you, Rosalind *querida*? You will not stand there and tell me that you do not quiver at my touch.' He took a step forward and slipped his left hand over hers, lifted it to his mouth and brushed, oh, so lightly, the back of it, his lips parting slightly so she could feel the warm moistness along her skin.

'No, please—'

Her voice was faint, as faint as her breath was tight. She could feel her breasts start to tingle, and the touch of his thumb at the base of her neck seemed to be washing down through the length of her spine.

'Please—'

Her voice was even fainter. The world seemed to be fading away. Reduced only to the touch of his thumb stroking her nape. Then, as he pulled her hand down towards him, he closed the space between them, and his mouth was not brushing her knuckles, but her lips, and a thousand sensations were bucking through her, leaving her weaker, fainter than she had ever been in her life.

Her eyes fluttered shut. She gave herself to the bliss of it. The bliss of feeling his mouth moving slowly, oh, so slowly on hers, and his thumb working at her nape. And he was kissing her still, and her mouth was opening to his, and there was a little moan sounding in her throat which seemed to make him move in closer on her, and she could feel the long, lean heat of his body pressed against hers. Her breasts were tight against him and his mouth was tasting hers, teasing and tasting, and she had no strength in her to do anything, anything but let him, and sink her body against his.

And then she realised dimly that his fingers had moved, that the sensation had shifted. Slowly, slowly, her zip was easing back, the cool air was touching her spine, and now his hand, warm after the cool air, its palm gliding down her naked back, was leisurely unclipping her bra as it passed on its journey to curve possessively, languorously, around the swell of her bottom and pull him into her.

As he fitted her into the cradle of his hips she felt an easing go through him, as if tension had been drained away, as if he had positioned her exactly as he wanted her to be.

But his mouth was still possessing her, and she was returning its possession, finding her breasts pushing against him, wanting to graze against him even while the palm of his hand was holding her tightly. Making her feel every long inch of his very, very obvious arousal.

Desire drenched through her. Debilitating, helpless desire.

Somewhere in the remnants of her logical mind she knew she must pull away from him, knew she must step back, recover her breath, recover her sanity and zip up her dress, pick up her evening purse and walk, with unalterable purpose, towards that lift and go—just go, go, go...

But not yet. Not quite yet...

He was kissing her more deeply now, opening her mouth and caressing within, taking his pleasure and his ease of her. And at her hips he was moving slowly, rhythmically, insistently...arousingly.

And, dear God, but she was aroused! It was flooding through her like an unstoppable tide, and she wanted, oh, she wanted...

She wanted him. All of him. Everything of him. Wanted the closeness of him, the lean hardness, the male, virile beauty of him—wanted him piercing her, possessing her. And she knew, with a deep, releasing flood of relinquishment of the last of her ebbing resistance, that she was going to have him.

He was a temptation too gorgeous to resist.

*   *   *

He took her to his bed. She had no memory of how she got there, of the distance from the terrace to his bedroom, of how the cool, dark sheets of his bed came to be beneath her naked back, her naked hips and thighs. She knew only that somehow, some time, he had undressed her, easing the loosened dress from her shoulders, sliding it down her body, her unfastened bra disgorging her swollen breasts, ripe into his waiting hands. She had arched back, gasping as he cupped them, then dipped his mouth to their straining peaks, shooting such arrows of ecstasy through her that she'd thought she must explode with pleasure.

But there was more pleasure yet to come—so much.

He eased her back down, coming down slowly over her, and he was naked, too. She did not know how, did not care—cared only that his hands were stroking her, arousing her, and his mouth was on her flesh, laving, and kissing, and seeking.

Her hair was loose, like a sheet of rich chocolate swathed across the pillows, and his hands were sliding in it, holding her with it as he reared over her, his thighs like iron either side of hers. Her back arched as he lowered himself into her, arched to meet him, her body ready, oh, so ready, to take him into her.

As he entered her she gave a little gasp, her eyes flaring, and he gave a laugh, a low, triumphant laugh, and slid harder into her, deeper, and again, and again. With each thrust her arousal climbed. Her hands were around his back, fingertips gripping him with a power she had not known she possessed as she arched to meet him, time and time and time again, each time a deeper penetration, each penetration a deeper pleasure, pleasure upon pleasure—until each pleasure fused, one into another, more and yet more, and her back was arching, and her neck, and each thrust took her higher, and higher, and her body was one whole fusion of pleasure that seared her whole body in white, blinding heat…

She cried out, and it was as if that was a signal to him. He thrust one last, ultimate time, and his body poured into her as she convulsed around him, spread beneath him, possessed utterly by him.

It was the light that woke her. Pressing on her eyelids with insistent brightness, drawing her back into the day. The new day.

Even after her eyes had fluttered open, so reluctantly, she went on lying there, quite immobile. She was spooned against Cesar, and she could feel his chest rising and falling in rhythmic slumber against her back. His breath was warm on her neck, coming and going with that same deep, slumberous rhythm. His arm lay heavy across her, folding her to him, holding her.

For a while, a long while, she simply lay there, feeling him holding her. She felt so warm, so cradled, that she never wanted to move.

But she must move.

The dream was over.

Anguish washed through her, making her bite her lip to keep silent. She must go back to the bleak reality that waited for her.

She'd been mad to stay; she knew that. Had known it last night—known it from the very moment when the last of her resistance, the last of her will, had simply dissolved away in the irresistible tide of passion he had let loose in her.

Dear God, if she'd known how easily he could sweep her away she'd never have been so rash, so insane as to have courted such danger all evening!

One-night stand. The phrase came to her chillingly—and yet, reckless as she knew she had been, she could not regret it, lying here, feeling his arm holding her to his strong, beautiful body, remembering every moment of their consummations—so many she had hardly known when one ended and the next began!—that had melded her to him, time after time. No, she could not regret anything—anything at all...

She would remember last night all her life! It had been a time out of time itself, a dream, part of the magical, glamorous evening that had taken her away from the crushing pressure that was the reality of her life.

For a little while longer she went on lying there in her blissful cocoon, making herself feel every moment of being so warm, so safe.

Moving away was the worst thing in the world. Easing her body apart from him so carefully that he would not wake. Inchingly she edged away, until she was disentangled, and then she slid to her feet.

She felt cold, oh, so cold, and not just because of the chill of the early morning.

She wanted to turn and look back at him, but she knew she mustn't. She knew that if she looked back she would never leave him—and she must. Now. Quickly.

Her eyes skittered around the room, spotting her evening dress carelessly falling off a chair, her shoes scattered nearby, her bra peeping out of the black chiffon folds of her dress—her panties half under the chair.

She felt the colour come and go in her cheeks as memory flooded back—

No! There wasn't time to think of the memories! Not now—later. Later she would remember last night.

After all, she would have a long, long time ahead of her in which to remember Cesar Montarez and the magic he had woven for her with his body.

Cesar stirred. There was something wrong. A moment ago there had been something right—something totally right. Something so right he knew he hadn't felt so right for a long, long time. Might never, indeed, have felt so right in his life before.

Rosalind Foster had been in his arms.

But she wasn't any more.

His eyes sprang open.

Instantly they lighted on her. She was standing with her back to him, her shapely, rounded bottom veiled from him by a pair of panties which he remembered distinctly he had removed from her very enjoyably last night. Her arms were behind her back, trying to hook her bra together. Her long chestnut hair was tumbled down her spine, getting in the way of her fumbling fingers.

She was obviously in the process of doing a runner.

For a second a rush of primitive emotion surged through him—echoing very tangibly in his loins. She was trying to leave him!

Almost he leapt from the bed to restrain her, the primitive urge to prevent the departure of the woman he had spent the night with almost overpowering him—he wanted her again!

Then, as she finally managed to fasten her bra, and bent to pick up her evening gown, he relaxed. Lifting himself onto his elbow, he let himself watch her instead.

It was very pleasurable.

In the morning light her body was as superb as it had been last night. A true woman's body, with curving hips and full breasts. Graceful and queenly. And quite fantastically beautiful.

He watched her as she lowered her evening gown so that she could step inside it, pulling its light folds up over her legs and hips, sliding her arms into the armholes and then pulling it up over her torso. Her hands twisted round again, and started to drag up the zip. And still Cesar lay there, watching her, his eyes flickering over her in silent appreciation.

Zipping complete, she stooped to scoop up her shoes, slipping them on her feet. Her hair fell in a glossy waterfall as she straightened.

'That,' said Cesar drawlingly, 'was a complete waste of time, Rosalind *querida*.'

She froze. Totally froze.

Then slowly, stiffly, she turned.

Cesar hauled himself lithely up against the pillows, lounging back, the sheet winding around his hips and thighs. His torso moulded powerfully against the bedclothes, and he looked lean, and honed, and very, very masculine. Rosalind felt emotion kick through her, just as she'd feared it would.

'And now,' he said invitingly, 'you can take it all off again and come back here.'

'Cesar...' Her voice was faint. Her eyes were as green as emeralds in the morning light. And wide and staring. Appalled.

'*Sí?*' he returned encouragingly.

'I—I...it's not a good idea! I have to go. I really do!'

'You know,' he replied, and his mouth was quirking, 'you said that last night—but you didn't go, *querida*—and you won't go now.'

Her face worked. 'Cesar—please. This isn't a good idea.'

He raised his eyebrows. 'So what *is* a good idea? That you simply walk out on me? After what we did last night? Just like that?'

'Um—isn't it the simplest thing to do? Isn't it for the best?'

He gave a laugh. It was light, but there was an edge to it.

'The best? Rosalind, *querida*, I will tell you what is for the best.' He paused minutely, then looked at her. Just looked at her. 'You are.'

His eyes held hers. She couldn't move, couldn't pull her gaze away from his.

'And if you think,' he went on softly, 'that I am going to let you just walk out of that door and go, you must be dreaming.'

He threw back the sheet and Rosalind, with a gasp, saw that he was fully, completely aroused. He smiled and walked purposefully towards her.

She couldn't move. All she could do was stand there as he walked towards her, his naked body bronzed and honed and so absolutely perfect that she could not believe a man could be so incredibly made.

He stopped in front of her. She dragged her eyes from his body to his face. His eyes had darkened, pooling with arousal. She drowned in them, feeling her body quicken, her breasts tighten.

He held out a hand to her.

'Come,' he said.

CHAPTER FIVE

CESAR lounged back in the padded patio chair, the movement parting the edges of the short towelling robe he had thrown on when he had finally finished making love to her. She could see the fuzz of his chest hair and, if she glanced further down, all too much of the naked length of a thigh.

His body was so strong... She found herself thinking. Remembering.

Warmth enveloped her, warmth and a blissful post-coital languor that made it almost impossible for her to move from where she was sitting on the chair opposite his, her feet curled up under her legs, wearing nothing but Cesar's discarded dress shirt from the evening before. Her hair tumbled wantonly over her shoulders.

She *felt* wanton. Deliciously so.

She reached forward for her coffee cup. How extraordinary to think that she'd sat here last night drinking coffee and thinking, really believing, that she would be going home without making love with Cesar Montarez...

I'd have missed the most incredible experience of my life!

Regret? How could she? All she could regret was how short a space of time she would have him. He had granted her a reprieve, taking her back to bed when her resolve had been to leave—leave while she had the mental strength to do so.

But now? Oh, now it was too late. Far, far too late.

Far too late for anything but to be grateful that this had been given to her. Too late for anything but to go on sitting here, hazed in happiness.

She went on gazing at him as she sat curled up, the coffee

cupped in her hands. His eyes were closed, face slightly tilted into the warm morning sun, which bathed its radiance down on him. In repose she could see the planes of his face, the high cheekbones, the long, long lashes, the slash of his nose and the sensual shape of his mouth, the dark, raffish shadow around his jaw. A breath of wind feathered the silky blackness of his hair.

Her breath caught, and she felt something flutter inside her, like something being born.

All my life. All my life I will remember this...

Her gaze slid onwards, over the tops of the bushes and trees and out—out to the dazzling sunlit sea beyond. The beauty and glory of Spain came over her again, and she remembered how she had first seen it, standing on the balcony of their room in that luxury hotel near Marbella. They had just stood there, both of them, and gazed in wonder.

Sadness tinged her eyes. No, she must not be sad. That time was past and her life had moved on.

Just as this moment would soon be gone.

But not quite yet.

As her gaze went back to Cesar's face she realised that he had opened his eyes a fraction and was watching her.

'I want you again,' he said softly.

They made love yet again. This time, at Cesar's instigation, in the shower. It was, Rosalind realised as he drove into her, as she splayed back against the tiled wall, water douching over her head and slick, readied body, the most erotically charged experience of her life.

And as she descended with long, shuddering spasms from her orgasm, she felt it was a fitting crescendo to her brief time with Cesar.

Was it the natural draining of her hormones after sexual congress, or the bleak realisation that now, finally, this magical interlude had come to an end that filled her with depression? Or was it that Cesar, refreshed now, satiated, had quite obviously moved on from the mentality of lovemaking.

He had stepped out of the shower, seized a bathtowel and wrapped it briskly around her, and then taken another one for himself. Now he was shaving, with swift, sure movements, legs slightly apart, wearing his towel like a low-slung sarong around his hips. He was totally focused on what he was doing, moving the razor with deft experience. She was combing through her tangled hair with her fingers, gazing at him in this strange, tuggingly intimate situation, trying not to feel wave after wave of depression batter through her.

It was over. Cesar Montarez was getting on with the new day. He'd done with making love, he'd been refreshed and revived, and now his busy life was ready to resume. Deals to close, people to see, orders to give, money to make.

And her life had to take over again, too. The dream had ended, right here in this luxurious bathroom, and outside the door she would have to get dressed again, put on her evening gown, and head across the lobby to be put into a taxi by Cesar—he would do that at least for her, she knew, not leave it to one of his staff to escort her off the premises. He would kiss her lightly, tell her that it had been great sex—or something to that effect—and wish her well. Then he'd step back, the taxi would move off, and she would leave El Paraíso for ever.

Sable would think her a certifiable idiot for accepting her dismissal so easily, but there was no way Rosalind was going to try and cling to a man who had taken her to paradise and was now returning her to reality. She was simply grateful for what she had had.

She would not be greedy, wanting more. She must not—even though inside she felt a hunger for him that she feared might never be satiated. But what was the point of that? He was not for her—not for any longer. Instead she would put a brave face on it—what else could she do? She'd had a wonderful, magical time. She had no regrets—how could she? Her only regret was that it was over, and she would never, in all her life, see Cesar Montarez again.

Something stabbed at her—pain and loss. That—*that* was the true price of a one-night stand, she thought sadly. Not the cheapness of it—but the expense. Far dearer than she wanted to pay.

She finished detangling her hair and got to her feet from where she'd been sitting on the rim of the bathtub. In the bedroom she busied herself dressing. It felt daft, as well as forlorn, to be putting on an evening dress at this time of the morning, but it had to be done. Just as leaving Cesar Montarez—for ever—had to be done.

A hand gripped around her heart.

But I want more! I want so much, much more! I don't want to go—I want to stay. I want to keep the dream. Just a little longer...

She zipped up her dress with angry speed. Well, tough, she told herself. You can't have him. It's over. There's only one thing you can do now and that's go gracefully.

She lifted her hands behind her neck, and started to plait her hair. It would dry on the way back to the café. It would crinkle dreadfully—but so what? She didn't need it to look good for anyone.

A longing went through her so powerful it was like a blow—for it to be twenty-four hours ago, for her time with Cesar Montarez to be still waiting for her. But she'd used it all up, that brief time.

It would never come again.

The hand gripped her heart again, hard and unforgiving. She felt her throat tighten.

The bathroom door opened. Cesar, stark naked, clean-shaven, was using a handtowel to ruffle his hair dry. His honed, muscled body made him look like a god. Rosalind felt her mouth go dry with longing.

As he set eyes on her he stopped dead. A frown creased his brow.

'What did you put that dress on for?'

Taken aback, she could not answer straight away. Then she said the first thing that came to her, guessing what his words must have meant.

'I…I'm sorry. I thought you were getting dressed as well.'

Did he mean them to go to bed again?

His frown deepened, as if her words made no sense.

'But why put on evening clothes? I will ask the hotel boutique to send up a selection of daywear for you—you can pick what you like.'

She shook her head, mortified. 'Cesar, that isn't necessary. Please, I don't mind going home in last night's clothes. It doesn't bother me.'

'Home?'

'Well, the café. I live over it. I get the room free. Señor Guarde likes someone on the premises at night.'

He walked up to her, took her shoulders, and turned her around. Then, with one swift, decisive movement he undid the length of her zip. Then he turned her back to him.

'Didn't I tell you, *querida*—' his dark eyes looked down dangerously into hers '—that this was not a one-night stand?'

She was floating. Floating right off the earth. Soaring up into the stratosphere.

Cesar Montarez still wanted her! He was keeping her with him! Oh, she didn't know for how long—she didn't care! All she cared about was that the dream wasn't over. She had a little longer to live in this magical world with the most devastating man of all time, who could melt her bones with a single touch...

She hugged her joy to herself in a haze of disbelieving happiness. Everything, *everything* was like magic! Oh, the magic would wear out, she knew—how long did Cesar keep his women? she wondered. A few weeks? A handful of months?

She didn't care! Whatever she got of him would be precious to her, and she would relish it, revel in it, as a God-given gift that she had never asked for, never expected— but had received, blessing on blessing, all the same.

And it was a blessing in more ways than one—as Cesar Montarez's live-in lover she would be safe from Yuri Rostrov. He was *persona non grata* at El Paraíso.

The final cause of her happiness shafted through her again. There had been only one cloud on the haze of her sunny bliss when Cesar had made it clear that whatever he wanted her for it was not a one-night stand...and that had been the thought of Yuri Rostrov and the money she owed him.

But even there she had been granted a reprieve! As unexpected as Cesar making it clear he wanted to keep her longer had been the thick envelope that had been handed to her as she'd made her way across the casino lobby out to the taxi waiting to take her back to the café to get her things.

'Your winnings, Señorita Foster,' the man had said with deferential politeness. 'From the roulette table.'

Wonderingly, Rosalind had glanced inside—and gasped. There had been a wad of notes inside! But how? Surely she hadn't been playing with real money? But the notes were real all right. Had she won then? She'd thought she'd lost— was she wrong? But surely she couldn't accept her winnings, not when it was Cesar who had staked her? She ought to tell the man there had been a mistake.

But the words had died, unsaid. Into her mind had sprung

the most wonderful, liberating thought. She knew exactly what she would do with the money! It would dissolve the last impediment to her enjoying this wonderful, irresistible invitation to share Cesar's life for a brief, blissful time. So she'd merely smiled at the man and slid the envelope into her evening bag, then walked out to the taxi, her feet as light as air.

On her way back to the casino she'd stopped off at the bank and paid all the money—far more than three months' worth of her usual meagre repayments—straight into Sable's account. Doubtless Sable would think she'd got it from her new rich lover. Rosalind couldn't help smiling wryly. But wherever it came from it should, as Sable had told her, serve to placate Yuri for long enough—until Cesar called time on her and she had to go back to her penny-plain life in the café.

But till that happened—oh, till then!—she was going to soar on wings of bliss. In the arms of Cesar Montarez, the most wonderful man in the world!

Cesar looked down at the woman lying asleep in his bed. A sense of deep satisfaction went through him. Rosalind Foster was proving ideal. It wasn't just that she was so stunningly beautiful—with the kind of beauty that he still found so beguiling that he hadn't even begun to be bored with it yet, even after six weeks—but also that she was the easiest-going woman he'd ever known.

She never threw tantrums, never made demands, was never pettish or sulky—was always sunny-tempered and co-operative. The expression in his eyes changed. Not that she was some kind of cipher—she could certainly argue with him, all right! But only when they were talking about world affairs, or culture, or history. His expression shifted again—when the was the last time he'd discussed such things with a woman? No dumb brunette, she!

As if subconsciously aware of his perusal she started to stir, her graceful rounded limbs moving slightly. Even though she was still asleep, her movement was sensual. That was cause of yet more satisfaction. Rosalind Foster was the most sexually satisfying woman he'd ever had. There was an ardour, an intensity about making love with her that he had never experienced with other women—as if she was able to draw him deep within her own searing experience so that he caught fire from the intensity of her heat. And burnt in the same sensual, white-hot furnace...

And afterwards... The expression in Cesar's eyes softened. Afterwards, when he held her in his arms—that was better than with any woman he'd known. She would cling to him as if she were welded to him, as if she clung to him for her very existence.

And that felt good.

Very good.

And there was something else about Rosalind Foster that made his affair with her so different from all his others.

She wasn't forever asking him for things! So many of the women he had known were always on at him to spend his money on them. Some were subtle, some wheedling, some seductive—but the purpose was all the same. To get him to open his wallet for them. But Rosalind was different. Oh, she let him buy her clothes, but she never went on about having nothing to wear or desperately needing a new handbag or other expensive trifle! She didn't even seem to like gambling. After that first evening she'd never gone near the tables, even though he'd made it clear he would happily stake her. But she never asked him for anything.

Of course he spent money on her anyway—especially clothes—he wanted to. He wanted to see her natural beauty enhanced to the limit with fabulous clothes. She looked such a knock-out when she was dressed up that it took his breath away.

He gazed down at her wonderingly. Was she really not mercenary? he pondered. If so, she was a novelty out here!

Perhaps he had simply grown jaded and cynical over the years, seeing so many women chasing money, wherever it was, whoever had it. Maybe these days he simply expected all the women he encountered to be devoted to getting and spending other people's money, including his. Picking their lovers for their wealth and what they could buy them, the luxury they could keep them in.

But not all women were like that…

And maybe Rosalind Foster was one of that rare breed.

He went on looking down at her as he slept, and something pulled at him.

He wished he knew more about her. It wasn't that she was evasive, precisely, about her background, more that she just didn't volunteer anything—even in casual conversation. He still knew almost nothing about her. His only surmise was that she'd come out to Spain with a man—

But that was obviously over now. History. So was her unwelcome association with Yuri Rostrov. He'd made his own enquiries and the man seemed to have left Spain and taken his dubious girlfriend with him as well, the one that had got Rosalind mixed up with Rostrov in the first place. Cesar could only be relieved—no way did he want those two coming near Rosalind again, or her having anything more to do with them. Just the memory of how he'd first seen Rosalind hanging on to those gangsters brought a bad taste to his mouth. But she'd vowed she wanted nothing more to do with them, had looked horrified at the thought, and he believed her. He trusted her. She had no links to Rostrov anymore. None.

He went on looking down at her, turning over his thoughts, wondering what he really felt about the woman lying there, who had brought such satisfaction to his life.

And then slowly, because he wanted to, he reached his hand out and drifted a finger through her hair.

She stirred again at the slight sensation, and then a moment later her eyelids were flickering open. As they lighted on him the expression in their sea-green depths touched something in him.

'Hello,' she said softly.

He smoothed her hair. About one aspect of his affair with Rosalind Foster he did not have to wonder—she was the most desirable woman he'd ever possessed. As he gazed down at her lovely face, her even lovelier body, he felt himself stir. He wanted to make love to her—but now was not a good time.

'I apologise for the early start, but we need to get going. I have to be in Mahon for lunch.' His voice was husky. He was regretting the need to be up and about on business already.

She smiled, lifting herself up against the pillows.

'I'm not complaining,' she said, in that smiling voice. 'I've never been to Menorca. Do you still think we can spend any time there?'

'I'm due back in Marbella for a meeting in the early evening tomorrow, but we can have till then in Menorca, *querida*,' he replied accommodatingly.

'That would be wonderful!' She smiled, but there was the slightest shadowing in her eyes. He knew what had caused it—mentioning Marbella.

It was the one place she didn't like going to—that and the Alhambra. The former didn't surprise him too much— Marbella was not to everyone's taste, and Rosalind had made it clear she preferred the quieter places on the coast, what few were left. Her favourite place of all, he knew, was his retreat up in the hills above El Paraíso. That she adored—and that, too, marked her out from his previous women, he mused. The likes of Ilsa Tronberg found the *castillo* he was painstakingly restoring far too remote and primitive—they wanted the flash fleshpots of the Costas, not the crumbling antiquity that was his own personal, private project. But Rosalind had gazed around with open pleasure in her eyes at the ruined, lonely splendour of the place the first time he had taken her there, and laughed off its current lack of luxury.

'It's wonderful!' she had breathed, and he had found himself telling her of its history, of his plans for it, to restore it as a beautiful remote hideaway. She had entered into his ideas, readily seeing the vision he'd painted for her. He had taken her all over—along the old crumbling ramparts and into the dim, mote-filled interior just crying out to be brought alive again. And she had stood by the tower window, gazing out over the valley below to the blue sea just glimpsed beyond.

But that Rosalind would not let him take her to the Alhambra *had* surprised him. She had already visited it before, she'd admitted, but it was not a place to see only once in one's life, and besides, it had been years since he'd last been there himself. He'd have relished taking her around the palace that was, to his mind, one of the greatest glories of Mediterranean civilisation—as well as one of its most romantic places.

But when he'd suggested it—weeks ago now, in the early days of their time together—she'd looked away and shaken her head, and seemed visibly reluctant. He'd let it pass and not suggested it again.

Had she been there with this mysterious man she had come out to Spain with? Had they lived in Marbella? Was that why she didn't like the place?

A stab went through him, and he identified it with a sense of shock. It was jealously.

That, too, was something different with Rosalind Foster.

He'd never felt jealous, never felt possessive of any of his other woman.

But the thought of Rosalind Foster in the arms of another man—however long ago!—made him seethe.

As he watched her now, getting out of bed, unfolding her tall, queenly body, and heading yawningly for the bathroom, he felt again that deep feeling of satisfaction go through him.

And a shaft of desire.

The siesta he'd promised himself after his business lunch in Mahon seemed a frustratingly long time ahead. For a brief, impulsive moment he felt the urge to follow her into the bathroom and ensure that her shower woke her up very, very thoroughly indeed. Then, with a regretful glance at his Rolex, he put the thought aside. He'd just have to wait until siesta time…

But he'd make up for it then. Frustration was always the best aphrodisiac.

Puerto Banus, the most expensive part of Marbella, was buzzing with beautiful people—as it always was. The tourists were there to gawp as well. If you wanted to see seriously rich people in action, thought Rosalind, this was the place in Spain to do it. The cost of property here was astronomical—and as for the price of the yachts moored in the harbour, she couldn't even begin to put enough zeroes on the numbers.

Not that she wanted to. She didn't like being in Marbella—it held too many memories.

But Cesar had business to do here, and she had made no demur when he'd told her they would have to stop over for a night before heading back to El Paraíso, further along the coast.

She'd have followed Cesar Montarez anywhere on earth.

Just thinking about him made her heart glow. These weeks with him had been a season in paradise.

She had never been so happy! Not even when she had first come out to Spain. For that time, even though she had been overjoyed finally to have arrived, had been haunted by sadness, the sorrow that was yet to come.

And come it had.

Her eyes shadowed and she shut away the memories—for what was the point in remembering? Remembering would make her sad, and that would simply waste this precious time she had now, with Cesar Montarez.

A hand squeezed at her heart. Pain was waiting for her again, she knew—the pain of loss. Oh, this loss would not, *could* not be so bad, for Cesar Montarez would still be alive, living his golden life, graced with yet another beautiful woman at his side, and then another, and another.

And she would be left far behind, with nothing but memories.

And the hideous mess of being up to her neck in debt to a gangster.

Cold fingers squeezed at her. She didn't want to think about owing Yuri Rostrov so much money. She didn't want anything of that ugly, sordid world of gangsters and their molls touching what she had with Cesar. Spoiling it.

There had been no sign of Sable or Rostrov—Rosalind couldn't help hoping they were still in the South of France, anywhere but Spain. She wished Sable well, despite the life she led, and would always be grateful to her for helping her out over her loan, but discovering she'd passed it on to Yuri had appalled her. She shuddered. Cesar thought she was free of the gangster, had nothing more to do with him. But what if he found out about her owing him so much money? Well, she bolstered herself, he *wouldn't* find out. There was no reason for him to find out. *She* would never tell him—no way did she want that crushing burden spoiling this precious

The Harlequin Reader Service® — Here's how it works:

Accepting your 2 free books and gift places you under no obligation to buy anything. You may keep the books and gift and return the shipping statement marked "cancel." If you do not cancel, about a month later we'll send you 6 additional books and bill you just $3.80 each in the U.S., or $4.47 each in Canada, plus 25¢ shipping & handling per book and applicable taxes if any.* That's the complete price and — compared to cover prices of $4.50 each in the U.S. and $5.25 each in Canada — it's quite a bargain! You may cancel at any time, but if you choose to continue, every month we'll send you 6 more books, which you may either purchase at the discount price or return to us and cancel your subscription. *Terms and prices subject to change without notice. Sales tax applicable in N.Y. Canadian residents will be charged applicable provincial taxes and GST. Credit or debit balances in a customer's account(s) may be offset by any other outstanding balance owed by or to the customer.

NO POSTAGE
NECESSARY
IF MAILED
IN THE
UNITED STATES

BUSINESS REPLY MAIL
FIRST-CLASS MAIL   PERMIT NO. 717-003   BUFFALO, NY

POSTAGE WILL BE PAID BY ADDRESSEE

HARLEQUIN READER SERVICE
3010 WALDEN AVE
PO BOX 1867
BUFFALO NY 14240-9952

If offer card is missing write to: Harlequin Reader Service, 3010 Walden Ave., P.O. Box 1867, Buffalo NY 14240-1867

GET FREE BOOKS and a FREE GIFT WHEN YOU PLAY THE...

Lucky 7

SLOT MACHINE GAME!

Just scratch off the silver box with a coin. Then check below to see the gifts you get!

YES! I have scratched off the silver box. Please send me the 2 free Harlequin Presents® books and gift for which I qualify. I understand I am under no obligation to purchase any books, as explained on the back of this card.

306 HDL D2AR   **106 HDL D33X**

FIRST NAME   LAST NAME

ADDRESS

APT.#   CITY

STATE/PROV.   ZIP/POSTAL CODE

7 7 7	**Worth TWO FREE BOOKS plus a BONUS Mystery Gift!**
🍒 🍒 🍒	**Worth TWO FREE BOOKS!**
♣ ♣ ♣	**Worth ONE FREE BOOK!**
🔔 🔔 🍒	**TRY AGAIN!**

www.eHarlequin.com

(H-P-08/04)

time with Cesar. Her brief, precious time. That, one fine day, would end.

For it would, of course. One day he'd realise he was bored with her, would see another woman to pursue, and Rosalind would be severed from his life. Not cruelly, not harshly—for he was not a cruel, harsh man—but for all that he would put her aside. Just as firmly as he had put aside that Nordic blonde when his fancy had lighted upon herself instead.

She wished with all her heart that it was not so. In her waking hours she felt the terrible temptation of daydreaming of a life in which Cesar Montarez was not doomed to become nothing more than a precious memory. Of a life in which she was part of *his* life, for ever.

She put such longings away. She must not allow herself to dream of such things. She would be no such thing to Cesar Montarez.

She was just the woman he took pleasure in for this brief time. One woman in a long, long line, she knew, and there was nothing she could do about it except enjoy the time he allotted her and make the most of being with him while she had the chance.

And that was why she would follow him wherever he went, do whatever he wanted—for the chance to stay a little longer with him.

Her breath caught—oh, but Cesar Montarez was everything she wanted! All she wanted! She still couldn't get over the way her life had simply been turned upside down—everything swept away by him! How had she come to be having this affair with him? This consuming, compulsive affair from which she could no more walk away than she could leap off a cliff and fly?

How was it that every time she saw him, *every* time, her breath caught and her heart turned over and she just wanted to gaze and gaze at him, helpless and enthralled? How was it that when he wasn't there, in the same room as her, she felt a yearning, a longing, just to see him again. Waiting for him to walk through the door.

It was everything about him—*everything*! The way his dark hair feathered on the nape of his neck; the way his dark eyes looked out at the world; the way the lines flared from his nostrils to the edges of that beautiful, sculpted mouth; the way that mouth would quirk and make her throat tighten; the way he moved, walked, with that feline ease; the way his hands, so beautifully shaped, would splay out when he talked; the way he stood still, leashed with that poised, powerful grace; the way his long, silky lashes would lower over his eyes as he glanced across at her…and looked, and looked…filled with desire for her…

She could feel her heart-rate quicken just thinking of him.

And when she looked at him, touched him, kissed him, made love with him…

Wonder broke through her. She had never known, never imagined just how incredible sex could be! Had never known how it could consume her, devour her, inflame her with a passion that was incandescent in its burning heat. Cesar Montarez could melt her with a glance, a touch, and she would make herself his irretrievably, passionately, devotedly.

'*Querida?*' The sound of Cesar's voice interrupted her blissful reverie. 'Have you finished making yourself beautiful yet?'

There was humour in his voice and his eyes flickered over her as she paused in the act of feathering on a final touch of mascara. She met his eyes in the reflection in the mirror as he stood lounging against the doorjamb, and felt, as she always did, that familiar thrill go through her that he was still here with her, still in her life—and she in his.

'Almost,' she answered. 'But don't rush me when I'm

doing mascara, or it will smudge, and then I'll have to start my eyes again from scratch.'

His teeth gleamed in a smile. 'You don't need make-up to look beautiful.'

She gave an answering smile. 'But it helps.'

Long lashes swept down. 'Oh, yes, *querida*, it helps, all right…'

There was a drawl in his voice that made her skin quiver.

The dark eyes went on washing over her.

'That dress,' observed Cesar, 'is spectacular.' His gaze took in the full glory of the sea-green gown, shot through with gold thread that shimmered in the light.

Rosalind felt a shiver of unease go through her, countering the delicious thrill that always went through her when Cesar looked at her in that particular, oh-so-speaking way that told her so totally, so utterly, that he desired her deeply.

He had insisted on taking her shopping that afternoon, telling her that Marbella was a show-off sort of place, and that anyway he wanted to see her in something new. The evening dress he'd bought must have cost him a fortune— nothing so sordid as a price-tag had been attached to it!— and although she couldn't disagree, knew that it did indeed make her look spectacular, she still did not feel comfortable about it.

That Cesar Montarez was rich was undeniable—but having him spend his money on her made her feel bad.

It wasn't just that he seemed to take it for granted that the current woman in his life would expect him to lavish expensive clothes on her, but that a part of her desperately wanted to accept. Oh, not because she wanted the clothes themselves—or wanted him to spend his money on her. No, it was because she knew—with that shiver of unease that would, if she let it, turn into fear—that unless she did her best, her very, *very* best, to look as gorgeous, as fantastic as she could, then her time with Cesar would be even more limited than it was going to be anyway.

So that was why she let him dress her in designer clothes, why she went endlessly for beauty treatments and fussed over her appearance—because she knew that she must look as good as she possibly could to hold his attention. The shimmer of fear went through her again. After all, she was surrounded by fantastic-looking women all the time now—done up to the nines, perfectly turned out in one designer number after another... How could she possibly hope that Cesar Montarez would not be distracted by one of them, and compare her unfavourably to those glittering birds of paradise that flocked to this expensive lifestyle?

She put the finishing touches to her make-up, checking one last time that she had done everything she could to make herself look good, and stood up.

Cesar was ready to go, looking as lean and lithe in his superbly cut tuxedo as he always did.

They headed downstairs. Cesar had booked a suite in one of Marbella's top hotels, and now they were heading off to wine and dine at one of the resort's top restaurants.

To her relief, it was not one that Rosalind knew. She didn't want to go anywhere that would hold more memories than she could bear.

This place was clearly extremely fashionable, crowded with expensive people. Nevertheless, Cesar was treated with kid gloves by the staff. But as they took their place at a table in the bar, Rosalind carefully sweeping her skirts as she sat down in the low armchair, she saw Cesar tense and look past the waiter who had just taken their order for drinks.

Rosalind followed his line of sight, and her stomach clenched with dismay.

CHAPTER SIX

SEATED sideways at the bar, wearing a mauve cocktail dress so short it almost showed her crotch, was Sable. And beside her, his back to the rest of the room, looking as heavy-set and flashily dressed as when she had first seen him, was Yuri Rostrov.

The dismay in Rosalind's stomach chilled to icy fingers as her two worlds collided.

She glanced covertly at Cesar. He'd recognised the gangster, no doubt. His eyes came back to her, and she forced herself to try and wipe the look of dismay from her face. Something of it must have showed, however, for he nodded briefly, as if acknowledging the reason for it.

He got to his feet.

'We'll dine elsewhere,' he told her. 'I don't want that scum anywhere near you.'

He held out his hand to draw her up, but at that moment Sable's gaze shifted slightly and lighted on Rosalind. Astonishment blitzed across her face, and she slid off the barstool.

'*Ros*, I can't believe it!' Sable's London-edged voice jarred in her ear. 'I almost didn't recognise you!'

She headed towards them, face alight—her gaze slipping immediately past Rosalind to Cesar. Her eyes widened.

'Sweetie,' she cooed, her voice slightly slurred, 'you jammy, jammy thing! So this is your gorgeous man! No *wonder* you couldn't say no to him!' Her over-made-up eyes roamed greedily over Cesar, then glanced back at Rosalind, taking in her designer gown and pricing it to the last euro. 'You *have* hit the jackpot! *Loads* of money *and* sex on legs! Clever girl!'

She glanced coquettishly up at Cesar, flicking back her long blonde hair with a full wattage smile of blatant invitation. 'Hi, I'm Sable—and *you*,' she breathed, the scent of alcohol on her breath, 'are just *too* hunky to resist. And I bet...' she leaned forward, pressing her long purple-varnished nails against his lapel '...you are just *dynamite* in the sack!'

She glanced back to Rosalind and murmured lasciviously, 'How about lending him to me tonight, sweetie? I could really, really do with a good Latin lay!'

She gave an inebriated giggle and moved to press against Cesar. He caught her wrist and held her off, not roughly, but decisively. His face was a mask.

Rosalind wanted to sink through the floor.

But no such mercy was allowed her. Instead, worse followed.

Before she could stop her, Sable was talking again.

'Listen,' she continued, opening her eyes the widest yet to gaze up at Cesar. 'I just want to say—' her false eyelashes swept up and down '—how really, really glad I am that Ros is with you. I told her she was an idiot not to sort herself out! Someone like you is the answer to all her problems!'

A small, killingly polite smile parted Cesar's mouth. 'Rosalind has problems?'

Sable opened her mouth, despite Rosalind's furious signalling with her eyes, but at that moment she was saved— and yet plunged into an even worse ordeal.

Yuri Rostrov was approaching them.

Automatically Rosalind dropped her head, hoping against hope he might not recognise her. Surely she looked different enough tonight from the way she had that ghastly evening? On the other hand, with Sable flagging her up like a spotlight, she didn't hold out much hope.

'Señor Montarez.' The heavily accented utterance of

Cesar's name was not a question or an acknowledgement, but a statement.

Of their own volition Rosalind's eyes lifted to the two men. Yuri Rostrov might not be as tall as Cesar, but his bulk made him seem bigger. Yet when her eyes slid across to Cesar she saw, in his poised, controlled stance, a leashed power that reminded her all over again of the impression he'd made on her when she'd first seen him. That Cesar Montarez could be dangerous when he wanted to.

He answered the gangster with a brief nod. Two males, thought Rosalind, squaring off, assessing each other—deciding whether to fight or pass each other by this time. She tensed automatically, feeling a rush of fear for Cesar. However dangerous he might look, he could be nowhere near as dangerous as a gangster...

'You're far from your home turf, Montarez,' Rostrov went on, in heavily accented English. Sable had moved automatically from Cesar, and was plastering herself against Yuri with a cooing smile. He ignored her. 'Or do you own this place too?'

'No—but I'm...well-acquainted...with the owner.' Cesar's tone was light, but Rosalind could hear the warning in it.

The other man nodded, as if he'd expected that answer.

'So, tell me—from your personal experience of the habits of the Spanish police—do they have this place under surveillance, too?'

There was the briefest flash of a smile, like a stiletto blade, as Cesar answered. 'Not yet, Señor Rostrov. But who knows when they might choose to take an interest? And if they do—' he gave a shrug '—even legitimate businessmen can fall under suspicion.'

'Unfortunate,' said Rostrov heavily. 'However—' he looked Cesar right in the eye, giving him his message loud and clear '—as a legitimate businessman myself, Señor

Montarez, I understand your concern.' He gave a curling smile, showing his gold teeth. 'Tell me, are your blackjack tables profitable these days?'

Something gleamed in Cesar's eyes. 'That depends. Some guests…get lucky.'

The gangster laughed, pleased to have made his point. He might have been thrown out of El Paraíso, but he'd made Cesar Montarez pay. Now he spotted another way of getting at him. His eyes moved on to the woman at his side, and Rosalind realised with a cold feeling that he recognised her perfectly well.

'Classy, Montarez,' he approved, but with a baiting tone in his accented voice. 'Very classy. She might look respectable, but you and I both know where you saw her first. For all you've spent on her, she's just a class-act whore—that's all.'

The fist came from nowhere. It connected with a sickening crunch on Rostrov's temple. He keeled over, hitting the floor with a thud that shook the furniture, and lay still.

Conversation in the entire bar area halted abruptly, and every head turned to stare.

Cesar's teeth bared in a gritted smile. He stared down at his handiwork. He'd reacted on pure impulse, and he didn't regret it. At the periphery of his vision he could see Rostrov's half-naked tart standing with her painted nails pressed against her mouth in shock. As for Rosalind, she was simply frozen immobile.

He glanced beyond her. A waiter was hurrying forward, but he was being overtaken by one of the discreet, but clearly visible bouncers. Ignoring the shocked stares of the other patrons, Cesar stepped up to the man and spoke rapidly, but quietly. The man glanced down at the prone, unmoving figure of Yuri Rostrov, clearly a whole lot heavier than the man who had laid him out cold, and raised his eyebrows in tribute.

'Nice shot,' he said in Spanish.

Cesar grinned. A real grin this time. He rubbed his fisted hand with the other one, his knuckles now feeling their impact with Rostrov's skull.

'Put him out with the garbage,' he said brusquely.

'I think perhaps, Señor Montarez,' murmured the bouncer, 'an ambulance might be more appropriate.'

Cesar nodded curtly. He turned his attention back to the two women. Time to dispose of Sable as well—but a little more gently. He didn't want her anywhere near Rosalind. He slid his hand inside his jacket. Taking out his wallet, he slipped out some high-denomination notes and handed them to her.

'Time to go,' he told her briefly. 'Preferably abroad. Portugal's nice this time of year.' He nodded at the waiter. 'This lady needs a taxi—see to it.'

The man bowed hurriedly and headed off.

Sable took the notes without blinking. Heavily lashed eyes opened wide at him and she gave him an expressive look. 'Portugal's *so* expensive,' she murmured plaintively. 'And Yuri could be really generous, you know?'

She sighed heavily at the prospect of giving up her unsavoury but cash-rich lover.

Cesar got the message. Silently he peeled off some more notes. She took them without a flicker, but he could see her assess the amount and find it persuasive. Worth giving up Yuri for and clearing out.

With a sidelong glance at Rosalind, who was still standing there looking choked, she said with another bat of her eyelashes, in an intimately low voice to Cesar, 'I'm just *so* glad Ros wised up and took up with someone like you. She's *such* a looker—I always knew she could do brilliantly if she just put out. With her looks she could pull any bloke, however rich! She was mad to bury herself like that—especially after she'd lived the high life once before! At least

I can leave her knowing you've fixed everything for her!' She ran a forefinger along the lapel of Cesar's tuxedo, leaning suggestively closer. 'I envy the knickers off her for having a bloke like you—money *and* looks! You just do not *know* how hard they are to find together!'

She gave a heavy sigh, as if life was harder than anyone could imagine for females like her. Cesar lifted her lingering finger away from him, his expression arrested.

'Let's not meet again,' he murmured, quite expressionlessly.

Sable gave a little trill of laughter and sauntered off, tucking away her money into her satin evening purse, her bottom wiggling provocatively. Cesar spared neither it nor the supine body of the unconscious gangster on the floor a glance.

He wanted out. Now.

He held out a hand to Rosalind.

'Come,' he said peremptorily. It was not an invitation.

He had things to ask her.

'So—that was the female who got you involved with Rostrov?'

Rosalind stiffened. 'I was not *involved* with Rostrov. I told you that.'

'Well, perhaps *involvement* is too strong a word for it.' The sarcasm was audible in Cesar's voice. 'I doubt he gets *involved* much with his whores!'

'That's a vile thing to say! Sable isn't a whore!'

Cesar made a derisive noise in her throat. He was angry. Angry that someone like Yuri Rostrov had come within a million miles of Rosalind. And angry that she had ever gone anywhere near him. Even as a favour to a so-called friend, who was no better than a *putana* and in no way deserved Rosalind's friendship.

'She doesn't walk the streets—but that doesn't stop her being a whore. What would you call her?'

Rosalind didn't answer, and looked away. She didn't want to think about Sable. Didn't want to think about Yuri Rostrov. Didn't want to think about anything to do with the whole horrible evening. And she didn't want Cesar talking about it. Not now, not ever. They'd left the restaurant and come back to the hotel. They'd eat in their suite, Cesar had said. Rosalind didn't care. She had no appetite—just a sour taste in her mouth.

She wanted Cesar to drop the subject. But he didn't.

'So,' he prompted, 'what would you call her? A slut, maybe?'

'I don't want to talk about Sable!' Her voice was tight.

'No? Well, she wanted to talk about *you*, all right.'

His voice had changed. There was challenge in it. And more—the same note that had been there the first time he'd seen her, offering her a lift and warning her against keeping company with East European gangsters. She'd told him then she was a fool, not a tart—she wasn't about to defend herself again over her own criminal folly!

She rounded on him. 'Look, I don't care what she said about me! Sable is not my bosom buddy!' Guilt stabbed at her for disowning Sable, but she couldn't bear Cesar thinking she shared her values.

'You just helped her out that evening, "babysitting" Yuri Rostrov—that's what you called it.' The challenge was still there. So was that note of disdain. 'And you should care what she said about you. You really should.'

She stared.

'What do you mean?' she asked slowly.

His dark eyes were veiled. A question had formed in his mind. He didn't want to ask it, but he had to. He felt it forming on his mouth, refusing to be silenced.

Demanding answers.

'Why are you with me, *querida*?'

Her eyes snapped in a frown. 'What?'

'You heard me. Why are you with me? What's keeping you here?'

He wanted an answer. Wrong. He *needed* an answer. Time to find out just what Rosalind Foster meant to him— what he meant to her. Something was lashing inside him and he needed answers.

She bit her lip, looking away.

'That's such a pointless thing to say. You know why I'm here,' she answered, her voice low.

'Do I? Show me. Show me exactly why you stay with me, *querida*.'

There was challenge in his voice. In his stance.

Her eyes went to him. He was standing foursquare in the centre of the reception room of their suite. Masculinity rippled from him like waves of dark gravity, sucking her to him. He was the most beautiful man in the world, the most breathtaking, the most devastating. His eyes glittered and his mouth was held in a taut, tense line.

Desire leapt in her like a tiger, taking her by the throat.

She knew right now *exactly* why she was here with Cesar Montarez.

Because she could not get enough of him.

Whatever else she wanted, whatever daydreams tormented her waking hours, whatever else she might so secretly long to be to him, she was at least this: the woman he desired. Who desired him.

She walked up to him. Felt the folds of her fabulously expensive dress rustle around her limbs. Felt the prickling in her breasts that presaged the onset of desire. Felt that desire seep out from the core of her being and start to fill her veins with its sweet, intoxicating addiction.

She could feel her breasts swelling, her nipples hardening. Feel the rush to her head, her body. Feel the heat spreading from her core, flushing outwards.

Like a fire. A flame running.

He watched her approach. Stood stock still. He felt his body surge as she walked towards him, this fantastic woman who turned him on, and on, and on...

She stopped in front of him. He could see her nipples standing out under the fine, expensive material of her bodice. See her lips part, the pupils of her eyes dilate.

'Show me,' he said.

His voice was low. It was not an invitation.

For one long, timeless second she went on standing there, quite motionless, while the flame ran within them both. Then, in a single fluid gesture, her hands went to the back of her dress and sliced down the zip.

The dress fell from her like a discarded husk. She stood in its folds, her breasts full and engorged, straining from their low-cut bra. Between her legs, a low, insistent throb had started up.

'This is why I'm here—' Her voice was low, the words almost a hiss—urgent, irrefutable. 'This is why.'

She held his eyes, held them with a twisting, writhing thread that held him to her, held her to him. Desire ran along the thread, twisting, writhing...

For one more long moment he went on standing there, challenging her challenge. And then with a jerking movement he reached forward, hooking his finger up under the central panel of her bra and tugging her towards him.

Excitement shot through her. Hot, vivid, searing.

He saw it flare in her eyes, and his eyes lit with savage pleasure. With a swift, urgent movement he used each hand to run up each bra strap and hook it down, over her shoulders, and then, just as swiftly, just as urgently, he peeled the loosened bra off both her breasts simultaneously.

Her breasts spilled out into his waiting palms, full and engorged. As he filled his hands with them she gave a sharp breath of raw pleasure, her head lifting back, spine arching forward instinctively. A low laugh broke from him and he closed his fingers over each pulsing nipple, scissoring them.

She gasped again, feeling the exquisite pleasure of his slicing stimulation. He pressed forward against her, feeling her back arch even more as she thrust her breasts into his relentless caress. He lowered his head to her ear.

'Show me more.'

This time it *was* an invitation.

And she showed him everything. Everything about why she was with Cesar Montarez. Everything. With all her body. And much, much more than that.

They lay entangled in each other's limbs, clothes scattered all over the carpet, on the long sofa that was all they'd been able to reach as the conflagration of desire had sheeted through them until they possessed each other to the ultimate degree.

Rosalind's body was damp with sweat. She was still wearing her stockings and suspender belt, but nothing else. Cesar was totally naked. His tuxedo lay in a crumpled heap on the floor.

They said nothing, still coming down from the inferno they had both bathed in, like salamanders writhing in the fire that would give them life. Beneath the palm of her hand she could feel the heated surface of his torso, the staccato rise and fall as his heartbeat slowly began to normalise. Her face was buried in his shoulder and he hung on to her closely, folding her half across him, their legs splayed together.

'*Dios,*' he breathed slurringly, as though taken to an exhaustion he had never before felt, 'what is it that you do to me?'

She could not answer, merely moved her mouth tiredly across the skin of his throat. They lay unmoving, wrapped in each other's embrace.

Cesar felt as if a hurricane had passed over him, through him, and he was only now emerging into the still weather on the far side.

But not calm weather.

There was something inside him—knotted still, tense still. She had given him satiation as she always did, and this time more than ever, almost more than his body had been able to bear, but the sense of deep, abiding peace that she brought to him this time was not there.

'Rosalind?'

His voice came from nowhere. He had not intended to speak, and yet he knew he was going to. Had to.

Again she did not answer him, but he felt her tense. He knew why. He had tensed, too.

'What did Sable mean—that you had problems I could solve for you?'

For a third time she did not answer. And this time the tension in her body was palpable. Then, finally, she spoke.

'Sable believed I needed a man. She considered my abstinence…unnatural.'

She was lying. He knew it. Knew it with his knowledge of her that had somehow, in the weeks they had been together, gone so deep it lay beneath his skin.

Something cold went through him.

As if she realised it, she lifted her head and looked straight down into his eyes.

'Cesar—why do you pay the slightest attention to what Sable said to you? I told you she isn't a bosom pal. She's just someone I know.'

'Someone you know well enough to want to "babysit" Yuri Rostrov for?'

His voice had that challenge in it again. It angered Rosalind. Angered her because Sable and her horrible, horrible gangster-protector were poisoning her rare, precious time with Cesar.

'I don't want to talk about her! I don't want to talk about that gangster of hers!'

And, above all, she didn't want to talk about her 'problems'—like owing Yuri Rostrov thousands of euros.

She peeled herself off him, feeling cold at her separation from the warmth of his body.

She felt bad. Bad that she had lied to Cesar. Bad that he was questioning her about a part of her life she wanted to have nothing to do with this magical, wonderful time with him, but which was reaching out to it, polluting it, poisoning it.

And as she got to her feet, realising that she was still wearing her stockings and her suspenders, as if she were something out of a porn magazine, she felt a wave of revulsion go through her—as if Yuri Rostrov's vile words had polluted *her*. Making her behave like the tart Cesar had first thought her—stripping off for him like that just now, and then coupling with him on the spot...

She made for the bathroom, locking the door, refusing to look at herself in the mirrored walls, simply peeling off her stockings and belt as fast as she could, and tossing them into a corner. Then she twisted her hair up into one of the hotel's courtesy shower caps and stepped under the sluicing water.

Ten minutes later she felt better. She'd overreacted; she knew she had. Cesar had hated that exchange in the restaurant as much as she had—why else would he have thumped Rostrov?—and it was her fault that it had happened. Her fault for knowing Sable in the first place. Her fault for being so hideously in debt.

She'd lied to Cesar instinctively about what Sable had meant about her 'problems'. She wanted to keep that side of her existence totally, completely apart from what she had with Cesar.

And what did she have?

The question formed in her mind as she stepped out of the shower, enveloping her body in a huge, fleecy towel and discarding the shower cap, shaking loose her hair.

What did she have?

She sat down on the stool in front of the vanity unit, staring at her reflection. Her long dark hair cascaded over her shoulders and her still fully made-up face looked incongruously back at her, where she sat with the towel wrapped around her like a sarong. She pushed back her hair with her hands and reached for her make-up remover.

As she steadily wiped the make-up from her eyes and face the question kept going round her head.

What did she have?

Sex, she thought. I have sex. Bucketloads of it. Fantastic shedloads of it. Sex like I've never known before. Will never know again. Sex that has blown my mind away and turned me inside out.

But it was more than sex.

Well, of course it was more than sex, she told herself impatiently, wiping a cotton pad over her eye with smooth, regular strokes. It had to be more than sex. Because why else would she feel as if Cesar Montarez was the most incredible man in the world—whether or not he was making love to her? Why could she not drag her eyes away from him? Why did her heart lift when he came into a room and she saw him again? Why did she want to just sit and stare and stare at him, drinking him in? Why did she crave him like an alcoholic craved whisky? Why did the thought of the day when Cesar Montarez would be done with her fill her with a dread that made her feel as cold as ice?

Why did she indulge in such futile, hopeless longings and fantasies about him—seeing herself at his side for all her life, his wife, the mother of his children...?

Because you're in love with him—

The cotton pad stilled in mid-air. She stared at herself transfixed, completely unseeing.

Her breathing had stopped. Her heart had stopped.

No!

Denial rang from her. No! She was *not* in love with Cesar Montarez! She couldn't be. She *mustn't* be! She just mustn't!

There was no *point* falling in love with him! This affair wasn't about love—it couldn't be. It just couldn't!

But it is. You're in love with him.

The words came again, relentless, remorseless. With all her strength she tried to push them away, unhear them. Refuse to admit them.

And then, as if a dam had broken, the flood overwhelmed her. She bowed her head, weak with the rushing emotions racing through her body.

She *was* in love with him! She was in love with Cesar Montarez! It poured through her, unstoppable, a drowning tide of emotion that swept her away.

The realisation was overpowering—as if day had suddenly dawned with a blaze of sunlight in the middle of the night. A second sun burning forth.

She sat and stared. Stared at her reflection, huge-eyed.

I'm in love with him. I'm in love with Cesar...

How long she sat there she did not know. It might have been two minutes. It might have been an eternity.

Love took time away and made it meaningless.

There was only one, slight impediment.

Cesar did not love her back.

As she went on sitting, staring at her reflection but not seeing it, she felt the chill, sobering truth lap at her feet. Cesar did not love her.

And why should he? This affair wasn't about love. How could it be, when it was only going to be temporary—as

temporary as all his other affairs? Not made to last. Timed
to run out, fade away, be replaced.

No, it was nothing to do with love…certainly nothing to
do with her unasked-for unwanted love…

He must never know!

Resolution fired through her. It was the only thing she
could do—never, ever give him a chance to find out what
she felt for him. He would not want her to love him—would
find it a nuisance. An embarrassment. Totally unnecessary
to what he wanted from her.

No, there was no point in telling him she loved him.

None at all.

They ate in the suite. Rosalind didn't bother to dress, simply
swathed herself in a heavy kimono Cesar had bought for
her at one point, its long, silk-lined sleeves trailing on the
ground as she ate.

It was a most flattering garment, even without the tradi-
tional high-waisted cummerbund. Instead she simply pinned
it loosely to one side, and let it fall over her body. As for
Cesar, he had merely put on his dressing robe, after clearing
away his clothes and hanging up her discarded dress.

Rosalind was glad. It had not brought good luck, that
dress. Guilt winged through her. It had cost a fortune, and
now she never wanted to wear it again…

Dinner eased the situation between them. The familiar
ritual of drinking wine, eating delicious and expensive food,
brought things back to normal, Rosalind felt. Gave them
both time to recover, to put aside that vile, polluting incident
with Sable and Rostrov.

They talked about history. Nothing to do with what had
happened in the restaurant bar. Only things that were long,
long gone and could do no more harm to anyone, living or
dead. They were talking of El Cid, that great medieval war-

rior, who had sometimes fought for the Moors as well as the Christian kings.

'All I know about him is from the Hollywood film,' said Rosalind. She was glad to talk about such impersonal things. Somewhere locked safely inside her was the discovery she had just made about her feelings for Cesar Montarez. But they were far too dangerous to do anything with other than keep them tightly locked inside a box. She must not open that box. It was too dangerous. Too pointless.

So instead she talked of history. Safe, dead history.

'It used to be on at Christmas—on TV. The ending was wonderful—so sad, yet so moving. Where they tied his dead body to his saddle and sent him out at the head of his troops—riding out of history and into legend.'

Cesar smiled wryly. 'For Hollywood, it was a good film,' he conceded. 'It glossed over a lot, but then a film must always do so. A film cannot be history—it can only be an expression of history. So you watched it at Christmas, did you?'

It was rare, incredibly rare, that she talked about herself before she'd met him, except in the most general terms, such as her love for history. To hear her mention her childhood was unheard-of.

'Well, that's the way I remember it. It was a very long film—good for winter afternoons.'

Cesar took a drink of wine. 'Did it make you want to come to Spain? Tell me,' he went on, not missing a beat, 'why will you not visit the Alhambra with me?'

She stilled. 'I…I… Well, I've seen it. I'd rather see other things, I guess.'

'Who with? Who did you see it with?'

Why was he asking her this? Why did he want her to tell him what he did not even want to know? Except that he *did* want to know it. He wanted, *needed* to know all about her— everything. Even her past lover.

So that he could discount him and stop agonising over him.

She took a forkful of seafood.

'Someone,' she answered. Someone who was gone, who would never come again. Someone it hurt too much to think about—even now.

Cesar looked at her. 'Someone you came to Spain with? Someone you left England with?'

She swallowed. 'Yes. Cesar, why are you being like this?'

Inside, she felt the box creak, as if the thing inside it wanted to come out. But she must not let it out.

He set down his glass suddenly.

'Because I don't know you, Rosalind. I don't know anything about you.'

His dark eyes looked into hers.

She dipped her head instinctively.

'There's nothing to know, really. I'm just very ordinary. The only thing special about me is you, Cesar.'

She wanted him to smile. Wanted to see that quirking tug at his lips that he did when she amused him. But he didn't. Danger pressed at her. If he went on asking her things he might find the box—the box she had locked so tight within her chest.

'Is it?' His voice was light. But she was not deceived. 'And why do you say that, *querida*?'

'Because it's true.'

'And why? Why am I special to you, as you claim?'

There was a probing tone to his voice. A challenge again. She felt danger prickle. She mustn't let him find out what she felt for him. It would achieve nothing—except her speedy departure from his life. Cesar Montarez did not want her in love with him. He wanted her the way he wanted all his women to be—complaisant, adoring, undemanding.

Certainly undemanding of his love.

'Cesar, I—I...'

She wanted to answer him. She really did. But she couldn't. Somehow she couldn't. She could feel tears starting in her eyes. She didn't know why, knew only that she couldn't sit here while Cesar Montarez interrogated her as to what he meant to her. It was too much, coming after that horrible scene with Sable and Rostrov. Too much, after that shattering new self-knowledge that she had had to crush down inside her, a secret never to be told—her love for Cesar.

'Cesar—' Her voice was choked, her vision blurring. She blinked and felt tears oozing, welling over her lids and catching in her eyelashes.

She dropped her head, her hand going to her forehead. She pushed back from the table.

'Please—I…'

She tried to get to her feet, but he was there before her, crouching down beside her and taking her hands in his.

'*Querida!*' His voice was stricken. 'Don't cry. Please, don't cry!'

Her head bowed over as she hunched forward.

'I'm sorry. I don't mean to. I'm sorry. But it's been such a horrible, horrible evening…'

At least she could say that. Nothing else, but that at least. He put his arms around her. Cradling her against him.

'Don't cry, *querida*. It isn't worth it. *They* aren't worth it. It's over now—all over.'

There was such tenderness in his voice that she wanted to weep out loud. A hand clutched at her heart. She clutched at him in response.

'Oh, Cesar!' she cried into his chest. 'You are the best, the very *best* of men!'

She felt him smile into her hair, then he got to his feet.

'Let's finish dinner, Rosalind *querida*. Then go to bed.'

She sniffed, and looked up at him with teared eyes.

'Yes, please,' she said.

CHAPTER SEVEN

IT WAS wonderful being back at El Paraíso. Though travelling with Cesar was bliss—except for Marbella—what Rosalind loved best was being with him in his apartment at the casino. It almost felt like home.

She wished she could feel that way for real about his *castillo* in the hills, a thousand years away from the developments on the coastline.

She loved the *castillo*. Had loved it from the moment she had set eyes on it, with its ancient, half-ruined walls, as Cesar drove around the punishing hairpin bends and precipitous roads that led back from the coast up into the hills.

She loved it not just because it was beautiful in its own right, perched up so high like an eagle's eyrie, but because Cesar loved it.

It was his place, she knew. The place he was at home in. The place that was his, his alone, and did not belong to El Paraíso. Something that would long outlast them, as it had outlasted so much history already.

Yes, she loved it—but she could not be at home in it.

For that very reason—because it was Cesar's home, where the heart of him resided.

And that meant it was not for her.

Instead she made do with El Paraíso—and that was an easy task. She felt safe here, safe from the sordid, horrible world of Sable and Yuri Rostrov—they couldn't reach her here. Not that there was any sign of either of them. Maybe Yuri had gone chasing after Sable—though it seemed unlikely. Whatever—she didn't want to think about them until she had to, when she would have to resume paying back

Yuri the gruelling remainder of the money she owed him, little by painstaking little. Till then she was free of him. And till then, all she wanted to do was revel in being with Cesar—while she had him.

He seemed to have completely put aside what had happened at Marbella. The strange mood that had come upon him in the aftermath of that ugly scene had vanished. He seemed to accept once more that she simply didn't want to talk about her life before she met him, to accept their affair for what it was, not seeking to probe her reasons any more.

And why should he? She strove so hard to be exactly what he wanted. Asking for nothing, accepting whatever he wanted to do. Wanting nothing but to ensure that her time with him was as wonderful, as magical as possible.

And yet…their relationship had changed.

Or rather—she had.

And she knew why. It was because she knew now that she had fallen in love with Cesar.

She tried desperately to hide it. Knew that Cesar would be appalled to know that a woman who was simply an ornament in his life, a graceful, beautiful, easy companion, in bed and out of it, was in love with him. He hadn't asked for that. Would not want it.

And because she wanted Cesar to have everything he wanted from her—because that way he would keep her with him just a little longer—she knew she must never impose her feelings on him.

And yet it was so hard to hide them…

Her love for him blossomed like a flower within her, touching every part of her—every part of her that touched him. She felt it like a sweet fragrance in the air she breathed, felt it lift and carry her on wings.

But it was a bittersweet thing. For while it made her time with Cesar glow like a jewel, it would also, she knew, exact a far harsher price from her than she had thought she would have to pay when the day came that Cesar Montarez replaced her in his life.

But there's nothing I can do about it. I love him—it is that simple. That irrefutable. That unchangeable. And when the pain comes I will have to accept it. I have no other choice.

But until that day comes I will stay with him. Accepting everything. Regretting nothing.

'So you finally made it!' There was humour in his voice, as well as mild reproof.

'Don't nag. I'm here, aren't I?'

Cesar tapped his watch. It clung damply to his wrist. His whole body was lightly sheened with sweat, and his muscles, pumped from weights, were sleekly contoured and beautifully displayed, thanks to his skimpy running top and shorts.

Rosalind flexed her shoulders. 'It's no good, Cesar—I'm useless in the mornings. I can't do a thing before breakfast.'

'Running would wake you up. It's the best time of day to be out.'

She cast him a jaundiced look. 'Yeah, right. And it's the best time of day to sit on the terrace and drink coffee—not hare like a lunatic between the palm trees.'

He gave a laugh and looped his towel around her neck, coming up to her. She caught the masculine scent of him and wondered how it was that a man who had just finished a two-hour workout could be so appealing to the senses. But she knew that the only thing on Cesar's mind right now was a hot shower and getting his feet under his desk. As for her, she would do a leisurely workout herself, here in the hotel's fantastically appointed gym, to loosen and warm up her muscles, and then head for the training pool. Swimming was her preferred exercise, not jogging.

He kissed her lightly, then let her go, unlooping his towel.

'Work hard,' he told her. 'Keep that fabulous body of yours in peak condition for me!' His grin took any sting from his words.

'Likewise,' reminded Rosalind, and her eyes ran over his corded body, which looked fit enough to win a medal just by standing there.

'For you—anything.' He smiled down at her. Then, with a brief, 'See you for lunch,' he loped off, pausing to have a word with Manuel, the on-duty instructor, before heading for the showers.

He felt good. The endorphin high from exercising was streaming in his body, and his tired but warmed muscles felt tuned, like a well-maintained engine. He would have liked to stay and watch Rosalind do her own workout—all that bending and stretching she did was very scenic!—but he had a lot of work to shift this morning. The joint project that Pat O'Hanran had proposed looked good—mutually good—and he was progressing it with all speed. The monthly accounts were due on his desk this morning, and he had his managers' meeting scheduled for this afternoon.

In his office, Mercedes, his secretary, handed him his coffee and drew his attention to any mail that he needed to know about. Nodding his thanks, he reached for the phone.

Life was good. Life was very good. El Paraíso was thriving, his new ventures looked more than promising, and the restoration of the *castillo* was proceeding apace. Soon it would be time to give serious thought to the interior décor. Rosalind had already made some enthusiastic suggestions, and he liked the sound of them.

Rosalind.

He paused in jotting down notes in the margins of the architect's report he was reading.

That was another reason life was good.

Very good.

He still didn't know what it was about her that made life

so good for him. Oh, he could go through the obvious stuff—she was fantastically beautiful, incredibly easy company, and unbelievable in bed! And since they'd come back here to El Paraíso this week she'd been even more devoted than ever—more ardent, more…more everything. The very idea of finishing with her seemed absurd—he had no intention of parting with a woman who was so perfect for him.

And she *was* perfect for him—quite perfect. Everything he could want. So why—a frown played in his eyes as he stared out of the wide window to the palm tree tops beyond—why did he even *think* of questioning that perfection?

Was he questioning it? If he was, why?

The frown deepened. Just giving thought to it seemed to bring it to life and make him realise that, yes, he .was questioning it. He knew he shouldn't, but he was. So why? Why couldn't hc just accept and enjoy the bounty in his life that was Rosalind Foster, the most satisfying woman he'd ever known?

But who was Rosalind Foster? The question came again, and he knew that that was what he was asking. He still knew so little about her—even after all his time together with her. Was that what bothered him? But why should it? He had no right to be bothered by the vague but persistent evasion she maintained about her past life. He had no right to be jealous of past boyfriends—however much he wanted to be! He'd accepted—of course he had!—that she'd come out to Spain with a former lover, and that that was why she didn't want to revisit old haunts like the Alhambra and Marbella.

Marbella. His mouth thinned. That had been a bad call. Encountering that scum Rostrov and that tart of his not been life-enhancing. The only good thing about it had been the chance to take his fist to Rostrov and lay him out cold.

Anger seared through him when he thought of what the man had called Rosalind. With no call for it—none.

Are you sure?

The doubt pricked in his mind like a mosquito bite. He splatted it away, but it whined back, biting again.

How much do you really know about her? She was no virgin when she came to your bed.

Well, why should she have been? The days when women were precluded from having a pre-marital sex-life were long gone—even among Spanish women. He didn't live like a monk—why should Rosalind have lived like a nun? And she obviously hadn't. She'd come out to Spain with a lover—but having one previous lover didn't make her promiscuous, let alone what Rostrov had called her.

The mosquito of doubt whined again, not leaving him alone.

A phrase hovered in his memory. Something that girl of Rostrov's had said. What was it? He paused, trying to hear it again.

'She was mad to bury herself like that—especially after she'd lived the high life once before!'

The frown came to his eyes again. Another memory intruded. The sight of Rosalind walking towards him the night she'd come to him at the casino—wearing a dress a million miles away from that tart-skin she'd sported with the gangsters.

He'd been totally focused on her breathtaking beauty, and his sense of triumph that she'd finally come to him—but now he thought about it again that had been no off-the-shelf frock. He didn't know the designer off hand—it was not something he paid much attention to in women's clothes— but that it sported a designer label he'd have gone bail on.

How could she afford a dress like that, working in a café?

Obviously she couldn't. So equally obviously she had once enjoyed a less constricting lifestyle than working in a café. Sable's words echoed in his head.

'—she'd lived the high life once before!'

Who with?

Lover-boy, it was obvious. Mr Mystery. The man she wouldn't talk about.

But, whoever he was, he'd had money. Money enough to buy her a dress like that black evening gown. Money enough to give her 'the high life'.

Well, so what?

With a rasp of self-exasperation Cesar picked up his fountain pen again. It was hardly a crime having had a boyfriend well-heeled enough to buy her a designer dress! *Dios*, hadn't *he* showered her with designer clothes? She had a wardrobe full of them, and looked a knock-out in every outfit!

Is that part of your appeal to her? That you buy her designer clothes?

That damn mosquito whined again in his ear, seeding its doubts.

He swatted it again. No, he wouldn't do this. Wouldn't pick away at what he had with Rosalind as if there was something wrong beneath the surface. There was no reason, no good reason for having doubts about her.

She might wear those clothes, but she never asked for them—and she certainly never hankered after jewellery, wouldn't even let him give her any…

No, he knew what his appeal was for her. It wasn't his money—it was *him*. She'd made it clear—totally clear—when he'd challenged her that night, in that angry aftermath at the hotel suite in Marbella, just what it was about him that made her stay with him. She'd shown him with every touch of her fantastic, incandescent body.

Just as she showed him every minute they were together, in bed or out—her visible pleasure in his company, her constant devotion to him, the way her eyes lit up when he looked at her.

That was why Rosalind Foster was with him. No other reason.

None.

He knuckled down to his work again.

'Señor Montarez? I'm so sorry. You have a visitor in Reception who does not have an appointment.'

Cesar looked up from studying the costings for his share of the O'Hanran project. Mercedes was standing in the doorway, looking apologetic.

'Who is it?'

'A Señor Rostrov.' Her face was expressionless.

Cesar stilled. His instinct was to give a decisively negative answer, but that might not be wise. Rostrov could be dangerous, of that there was no doubt, but he did not fear the man—not this far from his own territory. Rostrov could not afford to break the law here in Spain, or he would face deportation or worse.

So what did he want?

There was only one way to find out.

Slowly, he sat back in his chair.

'Show him up,' he told Mercedes.

The gangster entered the office a few minutes later, treading heavily. For a moment the two men levelled their gaze at one another. Cesar's expression was unreadable.

'Señor Rostrov,' he intoned evenly.

His uninvited guest gave a curt nod and sat himself down, unasked, in the chair opposite Cesar's desk. He spread his large gold-ringed fingers on the arms.

'I have a matter to settle with you—it concerns your...' Rostrov paused, then said deliberately, 'Woman.'

Cesar tensed.

The other man continued.

'I'm a generous man, Montarez, which is more than you should expect—' He rubbed at his temple consideringly, to convey the required message. 'So I'm going to go easy on you. If you want the English brunette, keep her. But sort this first.'

He reached inside his jacket pocket and drew out a thick, folded piece of paper, tossing it onto Cesar's desk.

Cesar could feel the adrenaline running in his body. It made him want to launch himself forward at Rostrov and beat him to a pulp. But he restrained himself. Something else was running in him—an emotion he could not name. An emotion that was starting to twist inside him like a newly hatched snake.

Slowly he pulled the paper towards him, unfolding it.

He read it at a glance, and as he did so he became completely motionless. When he looked up at Rostrov his face was totally expressionless.

Rostrov smiled. An unpleasant, gratified smile.

'Well, well, so you didn't know? Didn't know her dirty little secret. Didn't know that she's up to her pretty little neck in debt to me!' The gangster's voice was baiting.

He leaned forward, making his point. 'Let me tell you like it is, my friend. However classy they look, they like the high life, these whores, and they put out to keep it! Only sometimes they overspend—like this one did. Ran up credit she couldn't pay off. But I sorted it for her. And now you can sort it for me. Surely it's worth that much to stay between her legs? After all, it's what she's putting out for you for! Oh, don't worry—' he gave an unpleasant smile '--she didn't put out for me to meet her repayments—she's not to my taste. I like them blonde—like the one I woke up *without*!' he finished menacingly.

Cesar ignored the final jibe. It was an irrelevance that he had bankrolled Sable to do a runner. Everything was an irrelevance—except the piece of paper in his hand.

He saw his hand reach into his desk drawer, take out a key.

'You'll prefer cash, I take it?' he heard his voice saying.

Rostrov smiled complacently, his mission accomplished. He'd got his money—and humiliated Cesar Montarez into the bargain. The man had thrown a punch for the sake of a woman who'd made a fool of him.

Cesar went to his wall safe, opening the combination and counting out the money, handing it to Rostrov, all in the slow, deliberate manner of a sleepwalker.

The gangster slid the money inside his jacket and stood up. His eyes glanced around.

'Nice place, Montarez. But it has its expenses…when I come to visit.' He gave a fat, satisfied smile. 'Enjoy the girl,' he said softly. 'You've paid for her.'

He walked out.

Slowly, Cesar sat down at his desk, his face still completely expressionless.

On the desk in front of him lay the piece of paper that Rostrov had tossed down.

Damning Rosalind Foster without hope of exoneration.

Rosalind groped for the shampoo bottle and squeezed out a large blob into the palm of her hand before massaging it into her hair, leaning slightly out of the rushing water in the shower. She would need it cut again. As she worked up a lather with her fingers she made a face. All the endless beauty treatments and hairstyling she had to have to ensure she always looked perfect for Cesar might be necessary, but quite frankly they could be a total bore as well. They seemed to occupy so much time—and sometimes she could just wish the lot of them to perdition. But that was impossible—she couldn't afford to take any risk whatsoever that Cesar might find her less than one hundred and ten per cent gorgeous—from pedicured feet to freshly styled hair. She had to be as beautiful as she possibly could for him.

Half an hour later, as she sat at the dressing table in their bedroom, she knew she should be pleased with the results of all her labours. Dressed in a superbly cut cream linen shift, her lightly tanned skin flawless, her hair glossy and swept back from her face in a 'natural' look that had taken fifteen minutes of painstaking blow-drying, and with just a touch of eye make-up and lipgloss to bring out her features, she knew she looked as good as she could.

Her body felt taut and toned after her workout and swim, and she knew Cesar was right to nag her to keep fit. Not that she didn't enjoy it once she got going. And, after all, it was the only work she had to do these days. Her life was one of total sybaritic leisure, with nothing to do but make herself look beautiful—and bask in Cesar Montarez's company.

A perpetual dream time.

For as long as it lasted.

She picked up her cream leather clutch bag with its designer logo clasp, smoothed her shift over her legs, checked her appearance one last time, and headed for the door.

It opened before she reached it.

'Cesar!' she exclaimed. 'I'm not late, am I?'

He shut the door behind him with a sharp, decisive click.

He was looking very tall, she thought. And as she looked again at him she saw that his face was sombre. More than sombre. Closed.

Completely closed.

'Cesar—what is it?' Her voice was faint.

He did not move. His dark eyes were expressionless.

'Perhaps,' he said, and his voice was remote, as expressionless as his eyes, 'you would care to comment on this?'

His hand reached inside his jacket and drew out a folded piece of paper from the inside pocket. He handed it to her.

She took it with a puzzled frown, setting aside her handbag on the dressing table and unfolding the paper.

As she did so, she paled.

Her stomach plummeted.

'Well?'

Cesar's voice was terse.

She swallowed. Dismay flooded through her. Oh, no—no, no! Why did this have to happen! Why? She didn't want any part of it touching what she had with Cesar! She wanted to keep it far, far away from what she had with him—wanted to keep it a million miles away!

'How…how…did you…?'

Her voice failed her.

'I had a visit this morning. From our mutual friend Yuri Rostrov. Considering our last encounter, he was very civil. But then…' he paused. 'He had a matter of business to conduct with me.'

Cesar's voice was chill. As chill as liquid nitrogen.

Rosalind looked down at the piece of paper again. The one that spelt out in bald, horrible type exactly how much money she owed, and to whom. The zeroes blurred in her vision.

She lifted her eyes again.

'I didn't want you to find out.' Her voice was calm—quite calm, really. Which was surprising, given the waves of dismay washing through her.

Cesar smiled. It made her stomach plummet again.

'No? But I would have needed to find out very shortly, no?'

She stared at him, not understanding.

The smile came again, that curl of his lips that made her feel suddenly sick.

'You must have realised that now Rostrov was back, knowing you were living under my protection, he would come calling—looking to me to clear your account with him. Or did you imagine that because I so gallantly defended your honour—' the twist in his voice made her feel faint '—in Puerto Banus that I had seen him off for you?'

He gave a shrug. 'But it hardly matters. You can rest easy now, *querida*—I've paid him off for you.'

Her intake of breath was audible. 'Cesar—no!'

He smiled again, a smile that felt like a knife sliding across her skin.

'Cesar—yes,' he corrected her.

She shook her head. 'Cesar, please—don't be like this! I know it's a shock to you, and I'm sorry—I'm really, really sorry! I didn't want it touching us, spoiling things for us! I didn't want it to have anything to do with us! I didn't even want to think about it!'

'Really? The little fact that you owed Yuri Rostrov seven thousand euros was just something you didn't want to think about? So how, may I ask, were you intending to repay him? There was only one way, wasn't there?' His voice was harsh, condemning. 'The way you intended right from the start—to get me to pay it!'

'No!'

His lip curled again. She flailed on. 'Cesar, please— believe me! I never wanted you to find out—let alone pay it for me! Truly I didn't!'

She gazed at him entreatingly. But his face still had that closed, shuttered look. As for his eyes...

'Cesar...please...'

Her voice was faint.

'Yes...' he said drawlingly.

Anger was lashing at him like a whip, drawing blood, deep, deep inside. He'd been a fool. A blind, imbecilic fool! Thinking she was different. Thinking it was *him* she wanted, not his money. Yes, a fool indeed! But no more—*por Dios!*—no more!

'I like that, *querida*. I like you pleasing me—wanting to please me. Because you do want to please me, don't you? You've wanted to please me all along. You've been the most complaisant, attentive woman I've had—the most ardent, the most devoted, and certainly...' the drawl in his voice was like the blade of a knife '…the most eager between the sheets. I used to wonder why. Was it just me, I wondered, who accounted for such devotion? Could I really be that conceited? It seems I could—that night in Marbella you went to huge pains to convince me of the reason you were with me! And it was convincing, *querida*—very convincing.

'But perhaps,' he went on, in that same drawling, killing voice, 'you felt the danger of your friend Sable's revelation—those hints about you. What did she call it? Ah yes— your "problems". And now let me think—how did you explain that one away? Ah, yes—she disapproved of your lack of a man, that was it. Or should that be—' his voice hardened suddenly, pitilessly '—your lack of a *rich* man?'

Her throat was tight, so tight she could not breathe.

'No. No, Cesar—it isn't like that!'

He rounded on her. 'Then what *is* it like, Rosalind *querida*?' he grated savagely. 'Don't you enjoy having a rich lover? You haven't complained so far! You enjoy living here with me, enjoy all the clothes I dress you in, all the places I take you!'

'Of…of course I do!' She tried to fight back, but it was as if a drowning tide was rushing over her. 'But that's not what I'm here for! It's you—*you*, Cesar! That's why I'm here with you!'

'Ah, I see.' He exhaled slowly. 'So it's just the great sex? Is that what you're telling me? That's what you're sticking around for? Just the sex?'

His dark, deadly eyes bored into hers, and she could not meet them. Hers slipped away. She was terrified—terrified that he might see in her eyes the truth of why she was with him, that she was so helplessly in love with him she was powerless to do anything except cling to him desperately for as long as she could.

Even when he was throwing such vileness at her!

He saw her evasion—felt her lie shimmer between them. And a blow went through him that was mortal in its extremity. The bile rose in his throat, overpowering him.

Dios, but he felt like a gutted fish. One moment he'd been gliding in smooth, untroubled waters, and then, in a few brief, devastating minutes, his world had collapsed all around him. When he discovered the truth about Rosalind Foster.

Why?

The question was not why she had played him for a prime sucker so skilfully, but why, *why* did it hurt so much to find out?

He'd known venal women before—they were everywhere wealthy men were to be found.

But I didn't think she was one of them!

I thought she was different. I thought she was something more.

He tried to fight it, tried not to let himself be swept away on this floodtide of bitter anger. More than anger—something he wouldn't give a name to. Must not give a name to. So he tried to fight it—

So what if she is just another female like so many here, on the lookout for wealthy men? Why should she be different?

The answer came to him, clear and harsh and mocking.

Because you wanted her to be different, that's all! You were starting to weave fantasies around her, starting to think she meant something to you—that you meant something to her.

Well, you mean something to her, all right! You're the sucker who was going to pay off her debts for her! After all, who else was going to?

Anger lashed him again, dragging on his skin with iron fingertips. He crushed it down. What was the point of feeling anger, feeling pain, feeling anything?

She was speaking again, her face contorting, but he cut across her. He couldn't stay here any longer, with her bleating denial at him.

'I'm lunching in town,' he said curtly. 'Then I'm in meetings for the rest of the day. We are dining on board the *Aurora* with the Henriques tonight. The launch will take us out at eight.' His voice was clipped, impersonal.

Rosalind watched him walk out.

Pain clutched around her heart like a vice.

CHAPTER EIGHT

SHE spent the afternoon in the hotel's beauty parlour. Somehow it seemed the only thing to do. It was either that or go down to the beach and sit there, feeling like death.

What am I going to do? What am I going to do?

The question went round and round in head. But she knew there was only one answer. She had to make Cesar listen to her! She had to make him see that she had never, *never* wanted him to know about the hideous mess she'd got herself into! And she'd never wanted him to pay her debts for her!

Her heart contracted. Dear God, now she owed the money to *him*! How on earth was she to repay him? There was only one way, she knew. She would have to ask him for a job of some kind at El Paraíso—waiting at tables, receptionist, chambermaid. Anything. She'd repay what she owed him little by little, the way she had Sable, when she'd worked in the café.

And maybe, maybe, if she did that, then he would be convinced that she didn't want him for his money...

She was still in her kimono when he walked into the apartment. It was barely half past six.

'Cesar! You're early. I'm nowhere near ready!'

She attempted normality. That would be the best thing to do, she had decided. Be as normal, as reasonable as she could. Defuse all that cold, contemptuous anger that had been pouring off him when he had thrown her debts in her face.

'You look ready to me, *querida*.'

135

She looked at him uncertainly. His voice seemed normal. It didn't have that chilling quality to it that it had had before. She gave a flickering smile, trying to read his expression, his mood.

He saw it, and it amused him. Or would have had he been in the mood for being amused. As it happened, he wasn't. He was in the mood for sex.

And Rosalind was in just the right state of undress for it.

During the afternoon, which seemed to have stretched endlessly as his managers droned on during their monthly meeting, as his accountants went through the figures with them, his mind had been miles away. And it had come to some very rational decisions.

Very rational.

Rosalind Foster turned him on. Turned him on more than any other woman he had ever slept with. OK, so it turned out she was in it for reasons of her own, but now he had had time to consider it those reasons were no impediment to what he wanted out of her.

Sex. That was what he wanted from Rosalind Foster. He'd wanted it the first time he'd set eyes on her, cavorting with Yuri Rostrov, when he'd thought her nothing but a cheap tart. Well, he hadn't been so wrong after all, had he? Except that he could delete 'cheap' and substitute 'expensive'. Rosalind Foster had cost him a lot.

Something stabbed inside him, but he ignored it. Rosalind Foster had cost him more than euros. He'd paid in quite a different currency.

And now it was her turn to start paying him back for the money he'd shelled out to Yuri Rostrov. Paying him back for destroying his hope that at last, at last he'd found a woman that wasn't like all the others who'd clung to him.

But she'd turned out to be just the same as the rest of them, after all.

Something lashed around his heart. He wanted it to be anger.

But it wasn't.

He slammed it away and substituted another emotion. A familiar one.

A safe one.

One that was good enough for Rosalind Foster.

Lust.

Rosalind stood stock still as he walked towards her. There was purpose in his approach, and she knew what it was. The look in his eye was very, very familiar.

She felt the shaft of excitement slice through her the way it always did. She tried to stop it—sex right now was not a good idea. They needed to talk. Sort things out. Make everything all right again.

But Cesar was in front of her, reaching out and with the back of his hand softly stroking down the side of her cheek.

His eyes were dark, hooded, with an intensity in them that told her that he wanted her—right now.

'Cesar…' Her voice came, wavering. 'We really need to talk—'

She got no further. His mouth closed over hers, opening it and moving in on her with arrogant possession. His right hand slipped inside her kimono and started to play with her instantly ripening nipple. He stood there, legs slightly apart, one hand pleasuring her breast, the other spearing into her long loose hair, while his mouth feasted on hers.

Her eyes fluttered shut and she moaned, helpless beneath his ministrations as he steadily, relentlessly aroused her. His hand slipped away from her breast and she felt the ache of loss, but it skimmed down her silken flanks, beneath the heavy silk of the unfastened kimono, and his fingers glided inwards to part her thighs and stroke the satin flesh within.

She moaned again, deep in her throat, and she could feel him smiling into her mouth as his fingers grew more skilful.

She was flooding, flooding totally with the dew of desire, and her legs widened slightly of their own accord. She wanted more, more—

Suddenly, with an effortless flexing of his muscles, one hand curved over her bottom, the other hand around her back, and he hefted her up briefly into his arms, to take her across to the bed and lower her down upon the cover.

The unfastened kimono fell to either side of her, displaying her body to him. Fire licked all over her and she could feel her heart-rate racing, fast and shallow. She was in a state of extreme excitement, she knew, and it was blanking out everything else—everything except its own overwhelming, dominating need for satiation.

'Cesar—' She held out her arms to him, wanting to feel him come down on her, but he was discarding his clothes. Swiftly, concentratedly. Unknotting his tie and unfastening his shirt, shrugging off his jacket and then, with swift, sure fingers unbuckling his belt and disposing of the rest of his clothes.

She watched his lean, honed body reveal itself, and felt desire leap in her throat again. She reached forward for him, running her hands along the sides of his torso, revelling in the strength of his corded muscles, then moving inwards to clasp at his aroused, steel-hard satin length.

His eyes glittered, and he came down on her without finesse, filling her waiting body so completely she felt she could take no more. But she wanted more—still more.

Her hips arched up to his, increasing his penetration, and he drew back and plunged into her again and again, with each stroke building the excitement in her. Her hands were clawing at the bedcovers and her hips were twisting up to meet his downstroke, her head rolling on the pillow. Her whole body was taken over. Nothing else existed except this endless, mindless building of sexual excitement.

Her orgasm shattered through her moments before his consumed him, too, in one last, driving, relentless thrust, exploding within her own pulsing, convulsing flesh, drawing him in to her. The unbearable surfeit of pleasure roiled through her every limb, every nerve-ending inflamed and burning.

It took a long, long time for her body to subside, as if it had reached a heat that had been beyond endurance. As the orgasm finally ebbed away from her her body felt over-sensitised, over-aroused.

She felt her hips twist sideways, trying to free herself from his slackening possession. She was free, but still she felt the throbbing of her internal flesh, aroused too much. When he moved off her her sweated skin was suddenly cold.

She lay supine, her breathing slowly normalising, almost shivering, the black folds of the kimono beneath her. She didn't want to look him in the eyes—something was stopping her.

Briefly, so briefly, she felt his hand on her flank—but then abruptly, instead of folding her to him, as he always did after lovemaking, he simply levered himself up and got off the bed. Still not meeting her eyes. She watched him walk into the bathroom, not looking back at her. Saying nothing.

Her mind was blank.

She heard the sound of the shower, and after a little while she got up, wrapping her kimono around her. She wanted to go into the bathroom, too, but felt she could not. Instead she picked up his clothes from the floor, hanging his suit in the closet, folding his underwear and socks into his shirt, ready for the laundry.

She still felt blank. *I've got to talk to him,* she thought. But she couldn't think of anything to say.

* * *

They spent the evening on the yacht, *Aurora*, out to sea. It belonged to a French industrialist millionaire who'd recently stayed at El Paraíso, and who was now cruising the Mediterranean. It was a lavish affair, and the women were awash with designer gowns and jewels. Rosalind moved through them, aware she was drawing eyes because of her beauty and because of Cesar's company. Evenings like this, taking her place at Cesar's side, were nothing new; she'd been doing it since she'd first moved in with him. But there was something different about tonight.

Cesar was perfectly polite, perfectly affable—to her and everyone else. He laughed and chatted, part of the sophisticated crowd of wealthy guests, half talking business, half making innocuous small talk, in a mixture of Spanish, English and French, as befitted the cosmopolitan gathering.

Nothing much was demanded of Rosalind. All she had to do was smile and converse politely, inconsequentially, avoid the speculative look of males from time to time, and watch how much she drank. Champagne circulated endlessly, and then fine wines over the long and lavish dinner on the upper deck. She glanced across at Cesar. Was he drinking rather more than he usually did? Often he stuck to either white or red, but tonight she noted that he was drinking both, and he rounded off the evening with brandy as well.

She found herself hoping that the alcohol might relax him, make it possible for her to talk to him—really talk to him.

She had to bide her time, though. The motor launch back to the El Paraíso marina was hopeless—there were several other people present, for other wealthy guests had been invited to the yacht as well—and then there was the business of Cesar saying goodnight to them, as they made their way into the hotel. Finally she was walking at his side, up through the fragranced pathways towards the casino on the bluff above. Pools of light illuminated their feet at intervals, from cunningly set lamps along the way. In the bushes a chorus of cicadas chirruped incessantly in the warm night air.

Say something now, she thought. *Say something now!* Just say, Cesar, we need to talk—and start talking.

But she didn't. Instead she just walked at his side, not saying anything. Though he was not two feet away from her, Cesar seemed very remote. He had not taken her hand or put his arm around her shoulder. She could feel the distance between them.

They were inside the casino. The gaming rooms were still open, and business was brisk. Cesar turned to Rosalind.

'I'm taking a turn around the rooms. Go on up to the apartment.'

He walked away. For a moment Rosalind looked after him, then, with a small sigh, crossed over to the lifts.

It was at least an hour before Cesar came up. Rosalind had undressed, stripped off her makeup and showered, and she was sitting out on the terrace, reading desultorily. She hadn't put the kimono on. Somehow she didn't want to. Instead she was wearing Cesar's dark blue dressing gown and was curled up on one of the loungers, a table lamp from the living room beside her. An empty cup of coffee sat on the little patio table.

She heard the door open and close behind Cesar, and felt herself tensing. She heard him cross over to the drinks cabinet and there was the sound of liquid pouring briefly. He walked towards the open French windows, whisky glass in his hand.

He looked at her a moment. A long moment.

She met his eyes unflinchingly.

'Time for bed,' he told her.

She swallowed.

'Cesar—we have to talk. You know we do.'

Something moved in his eyes. 'Do we? What about?'

There was an edge of boredom in his voice.

'About the money.' It hurt to say it, but she had to. She just *had* to. 'I know you're angry with me, but you don't need to be.'

He took a sip from his whisky glass, watching her from the doorway. 'I'm not angry with you.'

His voice was indifferent.

She bit her lip. 'Cesar, please—don't be like this. It isn't the way you think.'

Suddenly, unaccountably, she felt her throat close. Tears pricked in her eyes. She tried to blink them away, but they came again.

Cesar didn't move. He went on looking down at her, framed in the doorway, whisky in his hand.

'Don't turn on the tears, *querida*. They fooled me last time—when you turned them on for me in Marbella, when my questions got too awkward for you to answer—but not this time. OK?' There was no anger in his voice, no emotion at all. He took another drink of whisky. 'So dry your eyes and come to bed.'

'Cesar—*please*—'

He moved suddenly, coming out towards her. He crouched down beside her, setting his whisky glass down. His eyes were dark. He took her hand.

'Stop this, *querida*. It isn't necessary and it's serving no purpose. We do very well together, you and I. Just because I found out you were lining me up to pay off seven thousand euros for you doesn't change that! I'm not about to throw you out just because of that! The amount is chickenfeed! Don't even think about it any more! But stop trying to tell me "It isn't the way you think, Cesar!"—just draw a line and close the subject.' He drew her to her feet. 'Like I said, it's time for bed.'

She looked at him uncertainly. She couldn't reach him. He'd made up his mind about her and that was that. And because of that she had a stark choice. She could insist on trying to explain—but with him like this she knew he would not listen. She could leave—walk out on him—call it quits. And she simply hadn't the strength to do that. Or she could stay and try and get through this, to the other side. Let him get over the discovery of her debts, do as he wanted and close the subject until it had ceased to be so sore within him, and then—then she could explain, get him to believe her.

She walked into the bedroom. Cesar followed her, shrugging off his tuxedo jacket.

'I need a shower. You, too.'

'I've just had one,' she answered.

His eyes rested on her. 'Have another one.'

She smiled uncertainly. 'OK.'

They needed somehow, anyhow, to break the unbearable tension between them. They'd made love in the shower countless times. It was a very erotic experience. But this time as they stood beneath the hot, pulsing water, as Cesar smeared her body with shower gel, gliding it purposefully over every limb, not saying a word, not touching her with his mouth, just palming gel over her breasts and bottom, and then lifting her up to impale her on his body, her spine pressed back against the tiles as she lifted her face into the water, gasping for air and ecstasy, it was too erotic. Too erotic when he disengaged, his body still fully aroused, hers shuddering in the aftermath of orgasm, and turned her around, pressing her palms against the tiles, parting her legs and pressing his own hands over hers, to pinion her body for him, then entering her from behind in strong, swift thrusts that brought her thunderingly to orgasm yet again—and himself as well.

For a moment they leant, collapsed against the wall, water pouring down over them. Then with a brusque flick of his hand Cesar cut the water and pulled out of her.

'Dry your hair,' he said, opening the shower stall door and reaching for a towel to give her.

She stepped shakily out of the shower, wrapping up her hair and taking another towel for her body.

She felt strange, dissociated. She had come down too quickly from the intensity of sexual arousal. She went into the bedroom, towel-drying her hair, wearing the other towel like a sarong, and got out her hairdryer. By the time it was dry again, a tumbled mass over her naked shoulders, Cesar was already in bed, a sheet pulled roughly across his hips and legs.

As she turned off the hairdryer and put it back in its drawer she could see that he was aroused again.

'Come here.'

His voice was low. It made her breasts prickle. She stood up from the vanity unit and walked towards him. She felt strange still. Sexual excitement was mounting again, but there was something different about it.

'Get on the bed.'

She started to peel back the bedclothes to go in beside him, but he stayed her with a hand on her arm.

'Lie down, *querida*. Face-down.'

His eyes had that dark glitter in them.

And suddenly, through the slicing sexual excitement that was knifing through her, another emotion forced its way.

'No!'

The word broke from her and she shook off his hand.

'No, Cesar! It's not going to be like this.'

The glitter in his eye intensified.

'Wrong, *querida*. It's going to be any damn way I like. And right now I want you on the bed, face-down.'

His hand rounded her bottom, moving across the twin globes, a finger hovering over the top of the cleft between. Again, she felt that knifing of desire.

'Spread for me, *querida*,' he said softly.

Almost—almost she did. Almost she succumbed to the raw, overpowering eroticism of what he wanted. To lie there naked for him, displayed for him, face-down, legs parted, so that he could arouse her, and excite her, and—

The word came into her mind. Ugly, and crude.

And undeniable.

Because if she did what he wanted her to—now, like this—that would be what he would do to her. Not make love, not even have sex. But something not even animals stooped to in their natural urges.

Because only humans could take something as natural, as magical, as God-given as sex, and make it something crude and ugly. And worthless.

She got off the bed, wrapping the towel around her body protectively.

'I said no, Cesar.'

Her voice was taut.

His face tensed, the glitter in his eye appalling her.

'The word is "yes", *querida*. It's the only word I want to hear from you. "Yes, Cesar. Please, Cesar. Whatever you want, Cesar. Whenever you want." Seven thousand euros worth of whatever I want…'

There was a tight, controlled savagery in his voice that made her feel sick.

'You said—you said just now the subject was closed.'

He smiled. 'Well, so it is, *querida*. Unless, of course, I have to remind you. Like I'm doing now. But I don't want to talk about the money you owe me. I don't want to talk about why you never mentioned owing it to Yuri Rostrov. Why you told me—*lied* to me—that you had nothing to do with him anymore. In fact, I don't want to talk at all, right now. So come back here, *querida*, and do what I want.'

She shook her head, her breath tight in her lungs.

'No.'

His mouth pulled. 'Why not? You've enjoyed sex with

me ever since that first time. We're good together—really good. That hasn't changed. And as for doing what I want— well, you always did that, too. I never knew a woman more accommodating than you, Rosalind, *querida*. So why balk now?'

She shook her head again. 'It's different now. You're making it different.'

His jaw tightened. 'No,' he said damningly, '*you* made it different. Not me. You. *You* were the one with the debts— not me!'

Her hands twisted in the knot of the towel where it strained across her breasts.

'Owing money doesn't make me a criminal! I never wanted you to find out about my debts! And I was never, *never* going to try and get you to pay a single cent of them! You don't have any right—*any* right at all—to make out that I'm some kind of whore! And that's what you're doing. But you've no right! I never asked you to pay a single euro back—you took that on yourself. I didn't ask you to! So cut it out—just cut it out! Because I won't put up with it!'

'Then don't, *querida*.' He met her defiance without missing a beat. 'Walk out—right now. Go out and pick yourself another rich lover. You've met enough rich men out there through me who'd be happy to take you on. Or you could always head for Portugal and pal up with Sable again.' His voice taunted her. 'You could work as a team.'

His words splintered through her. Each one needle-sharp.

She wanted to run. Run from the vileness of what he was saying to her. She wanted to throw herself at him, rage at him filled with fury.

But she fought past both urges. Fought to hang on to the truth that was deep within her. She loved him, and she would not let her debts—which were nothing, *nothing* to do with what she had with him—destroy this time she had with him.

She closed her eyes, standing there immobile as she let revulsion and anger drain from her. Then, opening her eyes, she lifted her head and looked across at him. He was still propped up on one elbow, his torso bronzed in the lamplight, his cheekbones stark, his mouth pulled taut.

'I'm not going to let you destroy us.' Her words were quiet. 'This time with you has been the most wonderful of my whole life. I didn't tell you about my debts because I didn't want to spoil it. I know it won't last for ever. I know you won't keep me long. I've known that from the beginning. I never thought anything else. I'm just one more woman for you. Up to now it's been wonderful. Magical. A memory I'll treasure all my life. And I'm not letting you ruin it, Cesar. If you think that all you've meant to me all these weeks is just as a wallet to settle my debts, then I don't want any part of it. I'll be your lover, Cesar. I won't be your mistress.'

She fell silent. He was watching her. Had she got through? She could not read his face. Then he spoke.

'That's good,' he said appreciatively. 'That's very good. Really convincing.'

Her heart sank. He believed nothing of what she had said.

'But you've been very convincing right from the start. And you've been playing me so carefully, haven't you? Never asking me for a thing. Making me think you were really different from all the other women out here. And what were you going to do, hmm, when crunch-time came and Rostrov came for his money? As you knew he must, sometime, once he knew I was keeping you. Trot out some heartbreaking hard-luck story about just how you came to be seven thousand euros in hock to a gangster? Something that sounded a whole lot more tragic than just running up credit card bills you couldn't pay off! And how come you got landed with those in the first place, hmm? The rich loverboy who brought you out here gave you a taste for the high-life? Was that it? That's what your pal Sable said you'd had!'

He drew a harsh, mocking breath. 'Well, you've got your high life back again, *querida*, and, like I said, I'm more than happy to oblige, and even pay off Yuri for you. But I think, I really think, it's time for a little gratitude.' He patted the bed again. 'So come and thank me, *querida*…very, very nicely…'

The glitter was in his eyes again, merciless, unforgiving—and as she looked at him hope died.

His gaze washed insolently over her.

She turned her head away, and started to walk towards the closet. She didn't know what she was going to do. Reach for some clothes—the first to hand? Go downstairs? Outside? Anywhere? It didn't matter. Nothing mattered. The weight inside her was crushing her. The sickness was choking her.

She slid open the closet door.

'What the hell are you doing?'

'Going.' Her voice came from very far away.

She did not look round, just reached inside the closet for a pair of trousers hanging there. The sound of his body jackknifing out of bed alerted her, and she twisted around just as he seized her shoulder. He took the trousers from her and flung them aside.

'You're not going anywhere!'

There was anger in his face. Whisky fumes on his breath. And something in his eyes that hollowed her out inside.

She backed away from him jerkily, dislodging his hand.

'Don't touch me! Don't—touch—me.'

She took another step backwards and bent to pick up the trousers, keeping her face turned to his, as if dreading he would move in on her again.

'I'm going, Cesar. I have to go.' She backed away again, till her legs bumped into the chest of drawers where she kept her clothes. She fished behind her, opening a drawer, pulling out the first top that came to hand.

He put out an arm to lean against the closed door. Quite naked. Superb in his nakedness. Something was dying inside her...dying.

'And the money you owe me?'

His voice was harsh.

'I'll pay you back. Little by little. Every month. I was going to ask you for a job at the casino, but now—' Her voice broke. She couldn't speak.

The lift of his eyebrow was cynical, his answer unspoken, and it angered her and destroyed her at the same time. She started to get dressed, her body moving mechanically. He stood and watched her for a moment. Then, with a rasp, he swore in Spanish.

'Enough of this farce! You've made your grand gesture! Over the top as it was! Do you seriously imagine you're going to waltz out in the middle of the night? Where the hell do you think you're going to go at this time of night? Head down to the town to see if another rich sucker picks you up off the sidewalk?'

She ignored him, stepping into the trousers and zipping them up. Her heart was thudding like a hammer and she felt sick. Really sick. As she pulled the top over her head waves of nausea started to go through her. Oh, God, she was going to throw up! This was all she needed! Desperately she tried to think what she'd eaten for dinner. Lobster? Had that been it? It had been something with seafood in it—and a far too rich sauce?

Salt ran into her throat. With a strangled groan she bolted for the bathroom, hand over her mouth.

CHAPTER NINE

IT TOOK her a long, long time to stop retching, and when she did she felt like death. Weakly, she dragged herself upright, hauled herself to the basin, and washed her mouth out half a dozen times, trying to clear the taste from her throat.

Finally she lifted her head and stared at her reflection. She looked like death, too. Ashen under her tan, her eyes staring, mouth pinched.

Was it the sickness in her soul made manifest? She didn't care.

A loud rapping at the door came again. Cesar had been thumping on it off and on for the whole ghastly session. She ran the taps one last time, flushed the loo one last time, and wiped her mouth and hands on a towel.

Then she walked to the door and unlocked it.

'What the hell—?' said Cesar, his eyes working over her. He'd got dressed in the meantime, pulling on jeans and a sweat top. His hair was dishevelled, his chin rough with shadow, and he looked haggard.

'It must have been the lobster,' Rosalind said hazily, as a sudden debilitating weakness sapped her. Her legs sagged.

He caught her instantly. She felt weak as a kitten, and she leant against him as he carried her to the bed and lowered her down carefully. The room whirled around her head, and for a ghastly moment she thought she was going to throw up again. She hoped not—there was nothing left to come.

'You should drink some water,' he said. His eyes were watching her, but she couldn't read what was in them.

He turned away and went into the bathroom, returning

with a glass of tepid water. He made her drink it, holding her up, and the feel of his body, holding her so carefully—but so distantly—made her want to weep.

He let her go as soon as she had finished the glass.

He got to his feet.

'I've called the hotel doctor. He'll be here any minute.'

She tried to shake her head, but it was too much effort.

'I'll be fine. It was the seafood.'

'Maybe.'

Her eyes rested on him. There was something odd about the way he'd spoken.

Awkwardness hung between them, tangible, like a rotting miasma.

The end of the affair, she thought, and felt a deep, abiding bitterness go through her.

She shut her eyes. The most bitter thing of all was that she could understand his anger with her. Feel his disillusion. How would she feel, in his situation, at discovering she owed so much money? Cesar Montarez was a wealthy man—and women who wanted a slice of that wealth were everywhere. It was the way of the world. Women made a living out of men who wanted to spend money on them—look at Sable. Whether you called her a whore or not was academic.

And what about me? What does it make me?

She'd enjoyed all the trappings of Cesar's wealth. Enjoyed the lavish lifestyle, the designer clothes, the first-class travel—swanning about in rich places with rich people. She'd taken it all, accepted it all. Oh, she'd said it was just so she could be the kind of woman he expected—perfectly groomed, perfectly gowned, an ornament for his arm, a beautiful woman to grace his side—because, after all, he was a wealthy man. Why should he put up with less?

The end of the affair… The words tolled in her brain like a funeral bell.

The doctor came, seeming to show not the slightest irritation at being summoned at such an hour. He was used to rich patients who demanded instant attention, even for trivial reasons.

Cesar left him to it. Rosalind watched him walk out of the bedroom, and felt his relief at being able to leave her at last. How he must be hating her, she thought—turning herself into an invalid just when he was denouncing her and she was on the point of bolting into the night.

The doctor spoke perfect English, and adopted that language straight away, despite Rosalind's opening greeting in Spanish. She ran through what had happened—the rich food, the wine—but glossed over the emotional storm that had probably triggered the bout of nausea.

The doctor nodded, and took it all in. And then, looking at her over the rim of his glasses, he said, 'And tell me, Señorita Foster, when was the date of your last period?'

Cesar stood on the terrace. He felt like a spring wound up so tight it must snap. His hands clenched over the iron balustrade, his shoulders hunched. He stared blindly out over the palm-tops to the sea beyond.

He wouldn't let himself think. Wouldn't let himself feel. Because it wasn't worth it. *She* wasn't worth it. A vicious tug pulled at his mouth. *Dios,* but she was good, though! That grand gesture of walking out on him—and then, just in time, that dramatic dash for the bathroom. The noises had been very convincing, but anyone could make themselves throw up if they wanted to.

It had been a clever move. Playing the sympathy card— *Be nice to me, I'm ill!*—and at the same time giving her an excuse to stay that wouldn't involve doing so on his terms.

His face hardened. Well, it would be on his terms from now on, that was for sure. She owed him and he was going to collect.

The night air brushed his cheek, lifting the hair on his forehead. Rosalind had used to do that sometimes, just run a finger across his forehead, feathering his hair…

Something clenched inside him. He forced it down. He didn't want to feel it. Only wanted to feel what he was feeling now. Anger. Contempt. Cold, hard feelings.

Safe feelings.

He went on staring into the night.

The doctor, when he emerged from the bedroom, coughed slightly. Cesar turned and walked back indoors.

'Well?' He might as well go through the motions. So might the doctor. He'd bill Cesar for his services, whether they'd been needed or not.

'I have administered a mild sedative. She should have uninterrupted sleep tonight,' the doctor said blandly, not spelling out what he meant by that. 'I will check her again in the morning. Goodnight, *señor*.'

Cesar nodded, and escorted the doctor to the door. Then, on impulse, he headed for the fire stairs. He wanted fresh air—a lot of fresh air.

Taking out the dinghy in the dark was tricky, but once he was out on the sea the night wind filled the sail. The dotted lights of fishing boats interspersed the night as he silently skimmed the surface of the water.

Thoughts consumed him. He let them rage through his head, let the wind take them. He didn't try to analyse them. What was the point? Rosalind Foster was as she was. Beautiful. Devious. Deceptive.

Dangerous.

Where had that word come from? Why?

How could Rosalind Foster be a danger to him?

She'd *been* dangerous—but she wasn't any more. Now he was on to her game. He'd keep her for what he wanted from her. All he wanted from her.

Sex.

Liar!

The word seared in his mind. The rudder jerked in his hand, making the little craft jib. Steadily he reset the rudder, and the boat calmed again. He went on heading out to sea.

Dawn was breaking over the Mediterranean. Fishing vessels were making for harbour. The sky was rose-gold to the east.

Cesar felt cold. Very cold.

As he nosed the dinghy into the marina, and moored it, he thought of Rosalind, asleep in his bed. He waited for desire to kick in him, but it didn't. Instead, an image swam into his mind, a memory of when he'd stood watching her sleeping the morning they'd gone to Menorca. He'd watched her for some time, taking in the tranquil beauty of her face in repose.

Something kicked in him. But it was not desire.

It was regret.

He strode up the pathway from the marina. What was the point of regret?

But he felt it, all the same.

As he walked into his apartment he paused. Something was different, but what? Then, as he went through into the bedroom, he realised what it was.

Rosalind had gone.

The coach journey back to England was long—endlessly long. But Rosalind spent the entire journey hunched into her seat, feeling numb.

Or sick.

The sickness was a real problem. She managed not to disgrace herself, keeping the bouts to service stops, but it was a struggle. Yet she was grateful for it, because it gave her something to focus on. Something other than what she was doing.

Leaving Spain.

It's been three years, she thought. Three years since I left England. As the coach made its way north-east across Europe the memories flooded back. How she had left England—flying first class, starting off in style, money no object! A sad smile crept across her face as she remembered.

Easier to remember those times, she realised, with a crushing pressure on her heart. Easier not to think of the times just past.

The vice crushed at her heart again, but she knew there was no point in regretting what she had done. Staying had been impossible. She had tried to win through to Cesar, and failed. She had not been able to convince him that her intent had not been malign—that she had wanted him for himself, not in order to use his wealth for her own ends. He hadn't believed her.

Nausea seeped into her mouth. She swallowed it down, breathing slowly and steadily, determined not to let it get the better of her. She stared sightlessly out of the window over the French countryside speeding by on the motorway.

And now she was beyond any hope of making him believe her.

Hardly aware of what she was doing, she slid her hand over her abdomen and went on staring out of the window.

At first, Cesar assumed Rosalind would return to El Paraíso. After all, she had left her entire wardrobe hanging in the closet. He had no idea where she'd gone, but he didn't much care. Who knew what friends and acquaintances she had out here in Spain? Her life was such a mystery that she could have holed up anywhere. She would, he presumed, lie low for a strategic amount of time, and then one fine evening she'd probably swan into the casino, dressed up to the nines, looking a knockout. Probably on the arm of another man.

She'd tried a lot of tricks with him. Maybe she reckoned it was time to try jealousy.

Would it work? He gave a private, cynical smile. Rosalind Foster might well find that she'd tried a gamble too far.

He was well shot of her. He might as well make the most of her grand gesture in doing a runner, and call her bluff on it.

The ache in his loins called his own bluff. He wasn't well shot of her at all! Oh, his hard sense might say that he was, but his body told him differently. His body told him, in the long reaches of the night, that it ached for Rosalind Foster.

And it ached not just for Rosalind pulsing with pleasure beneath him, but for her body curved against him, warm and soft, his arms wrapped around it, cradling her in sleep, sweet in his embrace. So very precious to him. So very dear.

His jaw tightened. No, he must put those thoughts away, those memories away. The Rosalind he imagined was not the real woman. He had built up fantasies about a fantasy. Rosalind Foster, the real Rosalind Foster, was nothing like the woman he wanted her to be. The woman who was going to be in his life—for ever.

And she never would be. He had found out in time. Found out what her real interest in him was. Whatever her protestations, nothing could take away the fact that, all through their affair, she'd hidden the truth. And when she swanned back into El Paraíso, to set her lures for him again, he would see her for what she was—not what he had wanted her to be.

But she did not return to El Paraíso.

She had forgotten the cold. The raw, damp cold that came up from the pavements and down from the clouds. She had forgotten the noise of London—the hiss of tyres in the rain, the rumbling of buses, the ceaseless churn of traffic.

Depression settled over her like a muffling cloud, and she welcomed it for it deadened all her feelings. The coach had arrived at some forsaken hour of the morning, and now she fought her way onto the Underground, heading north to the dreary suburb she had grown up in. As she emerged from the station everything looked grey, and colourless, and drear.

She stood there, clutching her suitcase, her back killing her after all those hours on the coach, her abdomen aching dully. She shivered in her thin jacket, hardly ever needed in Spain. She closed her eyes and tried to remember the heat, the warmth, the brightness and the light of Spain, but she was overpowered by the chill of England in the wet.

Someone bumped into her, and she murmured something in Spanish. The man looked at her oddly, and hurried on. Everyone seemed to be hurrying in the dull, grey street. She looked up and down the parade of shops on either side of the Tube station. Everything was exactly as she had left it.

She hefted up her suitcase and began to tramp along the pavement, heading north again.

It took Sandra two looks to believe her eyes.

'*Ros?* I don't believe it!'

Rosalind gave a weary smile. 'Yup, it's me. Can I—can I come in for five minutes?'

Sandra stepped back, opening the door wide. 'Don't be daft—come in and be done with it.'

As Rosalind stepped inside the other girl shot out a hand, halting her. 'How—how are you?'

Her eyes were searching. Pitying.

'OK,' said Rosalind.

The other girl just nodded, and led her down to the kitchen.

'Cuppa?'

Rosalind gave a wry smile. 'I haven't heard that word in nearly three years.'

'Sit down,' said Sandra. 'Meet Harry.'

The baby sitting in the highchair waved his spoon at Rosalind and blew a raspberry. She couldn't help but give a laugh.

'Hello, Harry. I've heard a lot about you.' She sat down at the kitchen table and leaned towards him. 'Your mother informs me,' she told the baby solemnly, 'that you are a genius.'

Harry blew another raspberry, and banged the tray of his highchair with his spoon.

'His mother,' said Sandra, turning round from filling the kettle, 'is totally right!'

'I can see G for genius written all over him,' promised Rosalind.

She sat paying attention to the baby while Sandra made tea, then sat down opposite her, pushing one mug towards Rosalind, keeping one for herself. Then she handed her son a toy, chunky coloured keys with a striped ball set in a socket for him to whiz around, and looked at Rosalind.

'How come you're back?' she asked, straight off. Rosalind remembered that Sandra always went the direct route. 'Your last letter—and it was a *long* time ago,' she inserted admonishingly, 'said you had no chance of getting clear for another year. So what happened? Did you get lucky? Hit the big time?' Her eyes sharpened. 'Meet Mr Right?'

Rosalind cupped her hands around the mug.

'No,' she said quietly. 'Mr Wrong.'

She didn't mean to cry. She really, really didn't mean to. But tears started running down her face and splashing into her tea.

It was the gala opening of the O'Hanran golf club. A posse of top celebrity golfers had been flown in for the opening tee-off earlier that day, and now they and the other glittering guests were continuing the celebrations at the brand-new deluxe clubhouse. Champagne flowed like water, and the five-star restaurant had produced a buffet worthy of a nineteenth hole so exclusive that invitations had been fought over.

Pat O'Hanran, well into the celebrations, came up and slapped Cesar jovially on the back.

'You can feel proud, m'boy. It's off the ground in record time.' He gave a crack of laughter. 'No *mañana, mañana* when you're on the job, eh?'

He slapped Cesar again, then took his elbow.

'I've been sent to kidnap you. Kathleen's orders. And you know I can't get out of those!'

Cesar went with him, but reluctantly. He knew why Pat's wife wanted him to come over. She'd have some female in tow, and would push her out in front of him. Then, when the girl failed to take, the Irishwoman would grill Cesar as to why, if he pleased, he appeared to be deaf, blind and dumb to anyone of the opposite sex. Cesar would simply tell her, politely but remotely, that work was keeping him too busy.

That, of course, was the whole point of the swathe of projects he had taken on. To keep busy. The O'Hanran golf resort was only one of the projects he'd gone for like a demon during these last months. The latest El Paraíso—two of them, on Menorca and in the Canaries—were well on the way to completion, and a third, in the Caribbean, was about to leave the drawing board. He was keen to get going on that one. It would keep him in the Caribbean for a season, and he could do with that.

Anywhere that wasn't Spain.

Anywhere he hadn't been with Rosalind.

His jaw tightened.

That she still had the power to influence his behaviour made him curse her. But then the woman had been a curse in his life—nothing else.

She had spoilt him for anyone else.

Oh, he had tried. Tried assiduously in that first, endless aftermath of her departure, as it had finally dawned on him that Rosalind Foster was not coming back to El Paraíso. That Rosalind Foster had walked out of his life for good.

He had deliberately decided to take up with Ilsa Tronberg again, and the blonde had been visibly triumphant. But when it had come to it he hadn't been able to touch her.

Her body was wrong. It was too thin, the bones too long, the texture of her skin too different, her hair too fine, her nails too sharp.

And the face was wrong, too.

And Ilsa Tronberg altogether—wrong, wrong, wrong.

She had not been best pleased when he'd finished with her a second time before even starting. He didn't care.

He'd taken out a tennis player next, over-wintering in Spain between competitions. She was American, bright and breezy, and with an honest, whole-hearted appetite for sex that he'd thought must surely do the trick. But Mae Gallison's body had been wrong, too. Her muscle tone was too strong, her breasts too small, her hair too curly. And her face had been wrong, too. He'd given his regrets, and left.

Leah Wong was exquisite. An investment banker with a top Swiss bank, she'd been a guest at Hotel El Paraíso, and Cesar had made her personally welcome over dinner. Her hair was like a raven's wing, her body like delicate porcelain.

But she was wrong, too.

He hadn't been able to touch her.

After giving up on Leah, he'd given up searching for a woman who wasn't wrong.

Now he was immune to all women. Even those hand-

picked by Kathleen O'Hanran, who'd told him to his face
that celibacy for a man of his age wasn't natural.

The one she had in tow now was no exception. Oh, she
was beautiful, all right, with peat-dark eyes and dark auburn
hair— 'The niece of my cousin's husband,' said Kathleen,
working as a linguist, and as intelligent as she was eye-
catching. Cesar smiled, and went through the motions,
danced with the girl, then handed her back to Kathleen and
Pat, and headed back towards the bar.

He got through a lot of whisky these days.

It helped to dull the pain.

The pain. He had faced up to it now, faced up to it in the
long, lonely reaches of the night—the pain of having fallen
in love with Rosalind Foster. Who had hidden all her debts
from him. Taken him for a fool. Let him pay them for her
and then walked out.

A memory, crude and ugly, of how he had treated her
that last night jabbed at him.

*Do you blame her for walking? You treated her like a
whore!*

He shot back in his own defence, vicious in his anger.

*What else was she? Strip away everything else, and what
else was she? What else could you call a woman who had
an affair with you and all the time was lining you up to dig
her out of debt?*

The other voice jabbed at him again.

*She said she didn't expect you to pay them! Said she'd
kept quiet about them on purpose...*

His mouth twisted.

*Yes, kept quiet about them until you were so hooked on
her you were putty in her hands. And as for all that prating
that she never wanted you to bail her out—think how she
promised she'd repay you! Well? Have you seen a single
cent come your way since she took off? And do you really
think you will?*

No, Rosalind Foster had let him pay her debts, and then, realising her game was up, had spouted her noble lines about refusing to be his mistress, refusing to let him 'spoil' their relationship, and promptly done a runner. She'd be off somewhere at this very moment, with another rich guy in tow. Living the high life at another guy's expense. Another fool like him...

A peal of laughter hit him as he approached the bar. High-pitched and artificial, grating on his ears. As he approached, the female who had laughed put her hand on the knee of a man sitting on a high bar stool. Cesar could see the man, but not the female's face. He looked to be about seventy or so, and the woman with her hand on his knee was well under thirty, he guessed—or at least was dressed as if she were. Or should that be underdressed? he revised, taking in the tight, short skirt hoisted round her thighs.

The female laughed again, and as Cesar reached the bar he glanced at her.

She was looking at him, her eyes alight with pleasure.

'Well, *hi!*' she exclaimed. 'I thought I saw you here!'

Cesar's mouth tightened. Great. This was all he needed.

'Hello, Sable,' he said heavily. 'Did Portugal not have charms enough for you?'

She gave a trill of laughter and leant against the elderly man's leg.

'And how!' she breathed. 'You know—' her eyes gleamed at him '—you did me a really good turn, sending me there. I found poor Hiram, *wasting* away in the Algarve. So I livened things up for him!' She popped a kiss on the man's wrinkled face. He smiled benignly at her. 'Hiram just loves golf—don't you, sweetie?' She addressed her escort, who might have twanged something like 'Sure do,' but Sable was talking again.

'So,' she said brightly to Cesar, her eyes swiftly scanning

the room beyond, then coming back to rest on his face, 'no Ros?'

Cesar's mouth tightened even more.

'We parted company some time ago,' he answered tersely. He caught the barman's eye and ordered.

'Oh!' said Sable hastily. 'Me, too—a Tequila Sunset, please!'

Cesar cast a glance at Hiram, who didn't seem to object to him buying her a drink.

'And for you, Mr—?' Cesar asked him, with more politeness than he felt he wanted to offer.

'Hackensacker,' pronounced the elderly man in a midwest accent. 'Hiram T. Hackensacker. Make mine a bourbon.'

Sable giggled. 'Isn't he a doll?' she said to Cesar.

'I can see the attraction,' he returned dryly.

Sable smirked again. 'He's got three married daughters,' she confided to Cesar. 'And they are just *so* mean to him. They won't let him have *any* fun! He is just *so* grateful to me for livening things up for him!'

Against his will Cesar felt his mouth quirking. There was an outrageousness about Sable that allayed his natural contempt for her lifestyle.

'Well, I wouldn't liven things up too much—he might not be able to handle it.'

She gave a giggle. 'Oh, I know just when to stop—don't worry! Trouble is—' her long eyelashes batted blatantly '—total sweetie though Hiram is, I just never quite seem to use up my natural…energy…these days. I could really do with some…exercise. You know?'

Cesar shook his head. 'No sale, Sable.'

She pouted, but not ill-humouredly. 'Well, you can't blame me for trying—now that you and Ros aren't an item! I'd never poach, honest. But, like I told you, packages like you don't stroll by every five minutes. No wonder I envied the knickers off Ros. So,' she went on, not drawing breath, 'how come you two split?'

He took a mouthful of whisky. Sable's elderly protector seemed untroubled by her attentions to another man, and was contemplating his glass of bourbon. Or possibly the array of golfing regalia on the wall behind the bar.

'Well,' Cesar said contemplatively, 'I owe it all to you, Sable, as it happens. That unforgettable evening in Puerto Banus.'

She looked puzzled. 'When you zapped Yuri? How? What did I do? I was really glad for her! I'd never have mucked things up for her!'

He gave a thin smile. 'Let's just say you—what is that English expression?—tipped me the wink. Made me realise there was more to her than met the eye.'

She still looked blank. 'I don't get it.'

Cesar shrugged. 'As it happened, Sable, I didn't know about the money she owed.'

Her eyes widened. 'Honestly—isn't that bloody typical of Ros! I *told* her to get you on-side as soon as poss, so you could sort her out with Yuri! How dim can that girl get?' She gave Cesar a narrowed look. 'Don't tell me you were too much of a tight-wad to sort it out for her? With all your dosh? Ros is *such* a looker you could at least have done that much for her! You were together *ages*.'

Why the hell was he having this conversation with this girl? Cesar thought disgustedly. Sable's morals came from the gutter.

And yet—

And yet he couldn't resist talking about Rosalind Foster. Couldn't resist the opportunity to break open the scar and make the blood flow again in the wound. He would pay for it—pay for it with dreams that night he wouldn't wish on his worst enemy. Dreams of wanting. Of losing.

He took another mouthful of whisky. Maybe it would help blot her out.

Sable was talking again. He forced himself to listen. He heard Rosalind's name mentioned again. Stabbing at him.

'—I mean, like, she'd had such a bloody time of it as well! She really deserved someone nice to get her out of it all. When I saw the two of you together I really thought she'd found it! And then you go and dump her after all she'd been through! That is really, really cheap of you, you know? I mean, don't you think it's really sad what she went through when she came out here?'

Cesar didn't like the accusing note in her voice. His expression hardened.

'Sable, maybe it feels like the end of the world for you when you get dumped by a rich guy, so you run mad with your credit cards, but—'

She put a hand on his chest, staying him in mid-sentence.

She looked at him with her overmade-up eyes.

'You don't know, do you?' she said.

CHAPTER TEN

ROSALIND crouched down, cleaning cloth in hand, rubbing away at the lumpy vinyl on the floor of the kitchenette. It was old and cracked, and no matter how much she cleaned it it still looked dingy. But she had no business complaining, she knew. The council had moved really fast, considering the waiting lists, and this little studio flat was a haven for her. OK, it was small to the point of being cramped, but what was the point of having a larger place? It would just mean more work keeping it clean, heating it and so on. And with money so tight, and all her time occupied by the only thing that was keeping her going, the studio suited her fine.

Memory flashed in her mind of a fabulous deluxe apartment with a seaview to die for in Spain, of an ancient hilltop castle high above the Mediterranean, of one luxurious hotel room after another—but she put it aside. What was the point of remembering that brief interlude in her life?

What was the point of remembering Cesar Montarez?

Pain gripped her and she fought it, as she had done all these long, long months back in England, away from him.

However it had ended, however painful it had been, however doomed, she still missed him, missed him desperately, as if a part of her was missing.

She would never see him again, would have to live with the knowledge that everything had come to grief, turned to ashes.

And yet it made no difference, no difference at all. Cesar Montarez was wrapped around her heart, now and for ever. However much she missed him.

Why can't love die?

Why can't it just wither away, turn to dust?

166

But it wouldn't. That was the worst of it. Her love for Cesar was so deep within her, so much a part of her, that it was with her always.

Even though all she had of him was memories.

And something even more precious...

The doorbell sounded, jarring in her ears.

It was probably Jan from next door. She was in the same boat as Ros, but seemed to do nothing but grumble about it—moaning away because the council wouldn't give her a new cooker, or provide a replacement for the DVD player she'd broken, let alone move her to larger accommodation. She liked to come and moan at Ros, slumped on the sofa, drinking endless cups of tea and eating biscuits and saying she had to lose weight or she'd never get a bloke.

Yes, well, thought Ros tightly, as the doorbell went again. Jan's last bloke had been a waste of space—no reason to think she'd get any luckier.

And you've been so lucky with yours, haven't you? Falling for a man who thinks you only wanted him for his money! The inner taunt made her lips tighten.

The doorbell sounded yet again. Rosalind sighed. Jan wasn't going to give in. She straightened up, tossing the floorcloth into the sink, rubbed her aching back and headed to the front door. It was shielded from the main room of the studio by a projecting wall, to give her a little privacy from callers.

She opened the door on the chain.

'Jan—it's not the best time right now—' she began.

Her voice cut out. Through the narrow gap between the door and the jamb she could see it was not her neighbour who stood there.

There was a roaring in her head. She felt herself slump weakly against the wall.

'Rosalind!'

Cesar's accented voice came like an auditory hallucination. She had not heard it for over a year. The last time she had heard it it had been ushering in the doctor to his bedroom, that last, terrible evening.

'Rosalind!' The voice came again. She blinked. It was not a hallucination. Nor was the man standing there.

He looks taller, she thought absently. Thinner.

For a long moment she stared at him through the narrow gap. Then, instinctively, she started to close the door.

A hand shot out, bracing against the door as he put the weight of his body behind it. The door jerked back to the full length of the chain.

'I have to speak to you!'

For a moment she just went on staring blankly. She felt blank all the way through. Her head was still roaring, but more dimly now. Mechanically she moved to unfasten the chain, pushing back on the door to release the strain. At first he resisted, then, realising what she was doing, he dropped his hand.

She opened the door.

It was Cesar. Yes, taller than she remembered. And thinner. His face was thinner. She studied it, with that same dim roaring in her ears.

There was a starkness about his face that was unfamiliar, but that was all. The rest of him looked just the same.

Devastating. Expensive.

'May I come in?'

His voice was as accented as she remembered—or was it more so? He spoke in a controlled fashion, but she got the feeling he wasn't controlled. Not at all.

A nerve was ticking in his cheek.

'May I come in?' he said again.

She shook her head. Saying nothing. Incapable of speech. Knowing only that she mustn't, *mustn't* let him into the flat, let him back into her life.

Something moved in his eyes. As if he'd just suffered a pang of something. She didn't know what.

'I need to speak to you,' he said. His eyes were dark, so

dark, looking down at her. She found herself thinking how long his lashes were. Far too long for a mere man.

The meaning of the words he had just said registered. They drew an echo from her.

'Cesar—we have to talk.'

That had been her line—but Cesar hadn't wanted to listen.

'If it's about the money,' her voice answered, 'you're out of luck. I can't afford to pay you back anything yet. But I haven't forgotten I owe you. You'll get your money back.'

Her words seemed to come from a long way away.

Cesar flinched. She wondered why.

She took a half-breath. 'Look—it's not exactly convenient right now. I'm pretty tied up—'

A sound came from the room behind her. A mewing sound.

She tensed. Cesar's eyes were focused on her.

'You have a cat?'

Her eyes flickered. 'Yes. Look, like I said—it's not convenient. So do you think you could—'

She didn't finish her sentence. The mew turned into a cry.

Shock shafted down his face. Before she could stop him he had walked in, pushing past her. He stood in the entrance to the studio, stock still.

'Por Dios—' he breathed.

With a deep, abiding feeling of inevitability that dampened down the roaring in her head, Rosalind walked forward. She crossed the room to the bed, tucked into the corner, and went to the Moses basket beside it.

The crying came again.

'It's all right, sweetpea. Mummy's here.'

She picked up the baby, swathed in a pink blanket, and cradled her. The wailing stopped.

Rosalind looked across at Cesar. Her eyes were as green as forest leaves. And quite expressionless.

'She's not yours. Don't worry. I picked up another rich sucker on the way back here.'

He flinched, visibly.

'Don't say that.' His voice grated.

She shrugged. 'Why not? It could be true.'

Something was knotting itself inside her, holding something down, restraining it. She had to keep it pinned down, had to subdue it. Whatever it took. Whatever it made her say.

He seemed to have gone white around the mouth.

'You weren't going to tell me, were you?'

Rosalind looked at him. 'No.'

She made the admission staring at him, green eyes stony, expressionless.

His face set. 'Why? Why not?'

Was there something else in his voice? She shut her ears to it. She wouldn't hear. She mustn't hear.

Instead she heard distant words drop from her mouth. 'Why not? You'd already paid out seven thousand euros on my behalf. That's quite a lot of child maintenance. And I'll be going back to work soon. There's a really good council-run crèche in this borough. I'm very fortunate. Don't worry—there's no father named on the birth certificate. No one's going to come chasing you for money.'

For a moment it seemed to her that he looked as though he'd been struck. Then, as her daughter realised that her rooting was not getting her anywhere fast, she let out a wail.

'She's hungry,' announced Rosalind. 'I'm going to have to feed her. Let yourself out if you're going.'

She was very calm about it all. Very calm about Cesar Montarez turning up on her doorstep after a year and discovering the daughter she had not been going to tell him about.

Very calm.

And it was important to stay calm. If she got upset she'd lose her milk, and then her baby would have to go on a bottle. And breast was best. All the parenting magazines said that, and so did her health visitor...

Her mind jumbled on, clinging to irrelevancies. Anything to stop herself being anything other than calm—very calm.

She sat down on the sofa, lifting her jumper and unfastening her feeding bra, then nestling the baby into position. As the infant latched on the crying stopped abruptly. Rosalind stroked her daughter's tiny head and murmured to her.

Her baby was her life now, her reason for living. Her only reason.

Then she looked up.

Cesar was still standing there, looking so tall and dark in her little studio that he seemed to overpower it totally. His dark expensive suit, and darker, even more expensive cashmere coat emphasised his physical dominance of the space.

She felt a bolt go through her, ripping away that paper-thin veneer of calmness she had clutched around her.

Cesar! Here! Now!

In the flesh...

And such flesh.

The bolt went through her again, and her eyes hung upon him, taking in every inch of his tall, lean body, drinking in his face, his features, his mouth and nose, his eyes...

His eyes...still splintered in shock.

Reality slammed back. Icing through her.

Well, she couldn't blame him for being in shock. It was a shock to find yourself a parent—she should know. She could still remember, as vividly as if he'd just said it, the Spanish doctor telling her, after he'd examined her internally, that he was pretty confident she was pregnant, and that that, not the lobster, had been the primary cause of her sudden nausea.

She hadn't believed him. Wouldn't believe him. Even when she'd done the mental sums in her mind and realised that, yes, she was overdue with her period.

'If you wish, I will return in the morning with a testing kit, Señorita Foster,' the doctor had told her. 'Be assured, I will be very discreet.'

But his discretion had been unnecessary—so had his pregnancy test.

She had packed and gone. It hadn't taken her pregnancy to make her go, but that had confirmed the need. Pregnancy had been the final nail in the coffin of her affair with Cesar. It would simply have confirmed even more that she was with him for what she could get out of him. Whether that was repayment of her debts—or life maintenance for his child.

Well, she hadn't been able to stop him repaying her debts, but at least she could stop him picking up the tab for his daughter.

That was what she had to hold on to now—that, and nothing else. Nothing else at all.

'There's no need to hang around,' she told him, in that same controlled, indifferent voice. So very calm. 'I'm not going to make any claims on you. And, like I said, when I'm earning again I can start putting money aside to repay you the money I owe you. It will take a while, but you'll get it all back. And if you don't—' she smiled thinly '—you know where to find me.'

A shadow passed across his face.

'I had to hire detectives to find you,' he said in a low, intense voice.

She made a face. 'I didn't know you wanted your money back that badly.'

His jaw clenched. The nerve in his cheek was working again.

'Do you know how I found you? The public registrar. Births, marriages—and deaths.'

His eyes rested on her. There was an emotion in them she could not read.

Refused to read.

'Deaths,' he echoed, his voice hollow.

His face contorted. 'Why? *Why* didn't you tell me? *Why?*' The words had broken from him. Vehement. Demanding.

She smoothed her daughter's head again, feeling the tiny body warm in her arms as she nursed.

'How could I?' she answered. Her voice was still remote, impersonal. 'You'd already said I'd be bound to trot out some kind of heartbreaking sob-story—'

With a sudden jerking movement Cesar's arm shot out sideways, his hand fisting. It impacted on the wall with a sickening crunch. His face was jagged with self-accusation. *'Por Dios!'*

The tiny mouth had stopped sucking. She didn't like the noise of her father hitting the wall with his fist. Rosalind soothed her cheek and relatched her on. She didn't look back up at Cesar.

'I thought you had simply got a taste for luxury and couldn't give it up,' he said, his voice still low. 'I thought you'd come out to Spain with a rich lover and he'd finished with you, but you'd got hooked on expensive living. I thought that was how you'd got into debt. I—didn't—know.'

His voice was bitter.

'Tell me...' His voice faltered, then went on. 'Tell me how it was. Tell me what the truth is, so that I understand...'

For a while she did not speak, only gazed down at her daughter. So tiny, so helpless. So unexpected and so very, very dear.

Then slowly, haltingly, she spoke as she cradled her daughter. Illegitimate, just as she had been.

The tale came quietly, dispassionately.

She had never been in the presence of her father. He'd refused to see her mother, even when she'd gone, begging, to his office. She'd been turned away, told to prove paternity in a court of law. When Rosalind was growing up she'd used to have fantasies of tracking him down, attacking him physically for what he had done to her mother. Her wretched, heartbroken mother, who had fallen in love with a total bastard and hadn't been able to bear the heartbreak of taking him to court to prove paternity—prove to the world what a total bastard he was.

But tracking down her father—attacking him, denouncing him, doing everything in her power to ruin his life as he had ruined her mother's—would only have upset her mother. So she had never done it. Instead she had become her mother's rock, her salvation. Her reason for living.

Her mother had depended on her totally. She had been the centre of her mother's existence. And the bond had been exceptionally close. With half her mind Rosalind had known so much closeness was stifling, that as a child, an adolescent, a young adult, she had carried too much of an emotional responsibility, to the point where it was a burden. But she had never seen it like that. It had simply been Mum and her—all the time.

And she had wanted so *desperately* to wave a magic wand over her! She had longed for a knight in shining armour to come riding up on his charger, fall in love with her mother and whisk her to paradise. But no white knight had ever come to the little terraced house in the dull north London suburb. It had just been Mum and her, living together, with her working locally as a secretary, her mother in a shop.

She had known all along that when she grew up, left school, went to local college, she could never leave her mother. It would have devastated her, taken away from her the one reason for her existence. And she'd been happy enough, knowing she was keeping her mother happy.

Until Barry had come along. She'd been out on dates often enough. Her striking looks had ensured her a ready supply of boys wanting to be seen out with her. But she hadn't taken any of them seriously until Barry. Barry had worked at the posh car showroom in the more upmarket

suburb next door. He'd been older than her, more sophisticated. And very keen to get her into bed.

When she was twenty-one he'd succeeded. He hadn't
been too pleased to find she was a virgin, and had told her
they were pretty boring in bed. Even so, he'd stuck with
her, and when he'd been offered a job managing an outlet
of the showroom company in the Midlands had invited her
to go with him. He'd even thrown in an offer of marriage,
because he could tell she was the type to want that sort of
thing. He'd been glad to have the chance to move to the
Midlands—it would get her away from her mother, who was
the clinging type and didn't like him.

And then, before she'd been able to give him an answer
on his proposal, her mother had collapsed. The diagnosis
had devastated her, drowning her in guilt because she'd
been so busy having her affair with Barry that she hadn't
realised her mother wasn't well. If she hadn't been so tied
up with him she'd have known that her mother was trying
to hide the fact that she was ill, and made her go to the
doctor earlier.

As it was, the cancer had been well advanced.

Forty-five. That was all her mother had been. Forty-five.
And all she'd had in life was her daughter.

The chemo and radiotherapy had been grim. Weeks and
months of it. Her mother becoming thin and then skeletal,
her hair falling out. But it had bought time. Precious time.

And when the doctor had taken Rosalind aside and told
her that her mother had perhaps nine months, a year, no
more, she had decided. Irrevocably, wholeheartedly.

The house had only been rented, and Rosalind had
chucked her job as a secretary at the local solicitor's and
made her plans. Her friend Sandra, just about to be married,
had been her co-conspirator. Together they had sold every
stick of furniture in the house and raised a lump sum. Then
Rosalind had raided her savings and added them to the pot.
And flexed her credit cards.

When her mother had come out of hospital she had been ready. So had the first-class air tickets to Spain, and the booking at a posh hotel in Marbella.

Her mother was going to have the time of her life—for the rest of her life.

And to hell with what it would cost.

For those last precious months she would live the high life.

As for Barry—well, a man who had told her with incredulous anger that she was off her rocker to blow so much cash on a dying woman was of no interest to her.

And she had blown it all—all the money she had scraped together and more. Running up debts on her credit cards with a ruthlessness that she hadn't wasted an hour, a second, regretting. She had lived the high life with her mother— shopping for them both in expensive boutiques, staying in the best hotels, eating in lovely restaurants, taking her mother to all the places in Spain she'd always wanted to see.

A wonderful swansong. A final time of being together.

While the cancer steadily ate up her mother's life.

The Alhambra had been the last place they visited. The last place where she had precious memories of her mother before the final end had come.

She had died in her daughter's arms, in the convent hospice that had taken her in for the terminal weeks of the illness.

Rosalind looked down now, at *her* daughter, so tiny, so beloved.

When she had been born she had known that her baby daughter would be her reason for her living. It would be hard financially, but she did not care. She would love her more than anything, anyone. It wouldn't matter that her daughter had no father—she hadn't had one either.

Her only regret was that her own mother had never known, was no longer there to love her grandchild.

'I've called her Michelle. After Mum.'

There was a tightness in her voice as she came to the end of her tale. She didn't want it to be there. But it was.

Carefully, very carefully, Cesar spoke. 'When I checked the registry of deaths and found your mother's record I went to visit the hospice where she died. The nuns remembered your mother well. Remembered you. Remembered your devotion. Your grief. I—I paid for a requiem mass for her. I—I hope you do not mind. It seemed...something...I could do for you, who put your life in hock for the sake of a dying woman.'

The tightness in her throat thickened. Like a garrotting band.

There was a footfall. A shadow over her. Over her nursing child.

'May—may I see her?'

Cesar crouched down. She saw his trouser material strain over the muscles of his thighs, saw the expensive cashmere coat pool on the shabby carpet. A hand, large, and tanned, reached out, and fingers tentatively touched the tiny head covered with fine, dark, silky hair. The hand seemed to be shaking slightly.

Something about seeing that large, strong hand touching that tiny, delicate head pulled at her. Inside, the hard, tight knot that had been winding around her, tighter, and tighter, pinning her down, gagging and binding her, began to loosen. She fought to pull the knots tighter again, like a tourniquet, cutting off all feeling. But as she looked down at Cesar's hand, cupping his unknown daughter's head, she could feel the bands unravelling. She tried to stop them, tried so hard...

His daughter did not interrupt her feeding for this moment in her life when her father first touched her. She went on sucking, strongly and rhythmically, her whole being focused on imbibing her mother's milk.

Cesar stared down at her, his heart crushing.

My daughter—

Emotion knifed through him. Pain, agony and joy—fierce, shining joy—all at the same time.

Something splashed on his hand. He looked up.

'Oh, *God*.' His face buckled. '*Rosalind*—'

He bent his forehead to hers. Blindly she reached and clutched at his hair, her fingers pressing into the nape of his neck.

A high, cracking sound came from her throat.

His arms came around her, folding her to him as he hauled himself up beside her, cradling her head against his shoulder.

'Don't cry. Dear God, don't cry. Don't cry.'

But she couldn't stop. A year's worth of tears were breaking from her. Pouring from her. Unstoppable. A torrent of tears, washing out so much, so much. Hardness and pain and hurt and loss. He held her, and stroked her hair, and murmured to her, sweet and Spanish, making her clutch at him again as the tears poured from her.

Until all her tears had gone, washing out every pain, every hurt.

'*Querida*,' said Cesar. 'Our daughter has stopped feeding.'

Rosalind lifted her face from the sodden patch of cashmere on his shoulder and twisted her head down. Michelle was staring up at her accusingly.

Then, with a shifting glance of blue eyes, the infant gaze moved to behold the other face looking down at her. She stared, unblinking. A tiny starfish hand moved.

Cesar placed one finger in her palm and the tiny fingers closed over it. A look of wonder passed across his face.

'*Hola, chiquita*,' he said to her. His voice was cracked.

Michelle considered her father. Then, with a jerking movement, she tugged his finger to her mouth and began to suck at it. A second later she rejectéd it in disgust, and opened her mouth to wail.

A laugh broke from Rosalind. Choking, but a laugh. A last tear splashed, and was gone. She sniffed noisily.

'I must give her my other breast,' she said. 'You have to keep the feeds even, or you get lopsided.' Her voice was tremulous as she imparted her new expertise in baby care.

A crooked smile parted Cesar's mouth as he shifted to let Rosalind free her other breast, taut and swollen with milk, and turn Michelle around to feed again. The wailing cut off as the baby's mouth closed over the nipple and the little starfish hand rested on the smooth, veined breast.

'Happy again,' said Rosalind.

The phrase echoed in her mind. She had said it at random, and yet suddenly it was there, between them.

Ringing true and sweet.

She lifted her eyes and looked at Cesar. She said nothing. She could not think, only feel. Feel, washing in wave after wave over her, an emotion so strong she could not resist it.

For a long moment he just looked, drowning in the green, green eyes that had haunted his dreams for the long year past.

But now she was real again, not a dream any more. Not a memory of loss, of pain, of hurt. And now that she was real again, now that he had found her again, he knew he must say what had to be said. To draw the poison between them, to heal the wound he had inflicted on her.

'Will you forgive me?' he said in a low voice. 'I was such a bastard to drive you away from me. But—' He took a deep, heavy breath. 'But when I found out about your debts something just snapped inside me! I felt gutted—as though everything we'd had together had been a lie all along. As though you'd just been playing me—taking me for a sucker, biding your time, waiting to sting me to repay the money for you like a total sap.'

He paused. 'It made me doubt everything about you. Remember everything about you. How you were such a mystery—you had no past, you would never talk about who you were or where you came from. So when I discovered about your debts, owing so much to that scum Rostrov, I thought the worst of you.'

'I didn't want it to touch us. Contaminate us. That's why I kept quiet about it. I tried to tell you that, but you wouldn't believe me.'

There was pain in her voice. It slashed at him like a knife.

'I wanted so much to be perfect for you,' she said sadly. 'I knew you didn't keep women long—that you'd be on to someone new soon enough, because hadn't you picked me up so quickly?—but I wanted to do the very best I could to make you want to keep me as long as possible.'

A bitter twist tugged at his mouth.

'I even became suspicious of that! Why you were so undemanding of me, so devoted, so…so perfect…'

'Until you discovered I wasn't perfect at all. And I couldn't bear it. I couldn't bear you being so angry with me. I couldn't bear…' She swallowed. 'I couldn't bear the way you were that last day. I couldn't bear it.' She paused, swallowing again. 'So I left you.'

The nerve ticked in his cheek again.

'I couldn't believe you'd gone,' he said. His eyes had a bleakness in them. 'I kept waiting for you to come back. I knew you would. I was certain of it—I was that arrogant. But you didn't. And day by day, week by week, month by month, I had to accept that you were not coming back to me. That I had driven you away.'

He paused. 'I tried to tell myself it was for the best—but I was lying. I missed you. Missed you in the day, and in the night. No other woman filled the space that you had filled.'

'You had other women?' Her voice was sharper than she'd meant, as sharp as the knife stabbing into her heart at his admission.

'I tried,' he said. 'But I couldn't. They weren't you. Each one was beautiful, each one was…not you.'

He stared sightlessly into the past he had just walked out of.

'Everything in the world was…not you.'

He was silent a moment, his face stark. And then, in a strained voice, he said, 'When—when did you know you were pregnant?'

She pressed her lips together, looking down at his daughter nursing at her breast.

'I never even suspected,' she admitted. 'It was that doctor who spotted it. He thought there might be another reason why I was so nauseous—and he was right. Just the possibility of it meant I knew I had to go—you'd have hated me even more, thinking I'd done it on purpose to get some kind of financial commitment from you. So I knew I could never tell you.'

A harsh sound came from him.

'*Dios*—if I hadn't tracked you down…' He sounded anguished, and Rosalind's heart squeezed. 'I would have lost my child as well as you…'

There was something in his voice that stabbed her.

'I'm sorry,' she said. 'I'm so sorry, Cesar.'

She felt the tears begin to come again, and his arm tightened around her. She felt his warmth, his strength, protecting and sheltering her. He cupped her cheek and she leant into his strong, safe hand.

'No, you have nothing to apologise about. Nothing! I drove you away with my vileness to you that last day! No more tears. Not now, not ever. You have shed your tears, *querida*, for your mother, and for me, and I will not let you shed one more. Not one more.'

He leant and kissed her. Very gently, very softly.

'I love you,' he told her. 'I loved you then, and was too blind to know it.'

She searched his eyes. 'I ask for nothing. Truly.'

'You have everything that I can give you,' he told her.

'Everything that my heart possesses. My life, my love, my soul.'

And he kissed her again.

'You realise,' Cesar said later, as he stood gazing down at Michelle, asleep in her Moses basket, while Rosalind made coffee, 'that I owe a debt of eternal gratitude to Sable.'

She stopped in the act of pouring water over the instant granules.

'Sable?'

He cast a last look at his sleeping daughter and walked towards the kitchenette. He still looked too tall for the flat, thought Rosalind, even now he had discarded his overpowering cashmere overcoat.

'She told me about your mother,' he said.

'*Sable* did?'

He gave a grating laugh.

'She laid into me and gave me an earful. I...I didn't believe her at first. I thought it might indeed be nothing more than a sob-story that you and she had concocted together. I was half expecting her to add that the only reason she turned over more men than hot dinners was because she was keeping her aged grandparents in their ancestral home! But she got angry when I expressed my scepticism, and swore blind by you. Told me to get on my bike and check it out!'

A pang went through Rosalind. Sable had turned up trumps after all. A wave of gratitude washed through her.

A thought struck her. 'When did you see her again? I thought you'd sent her off to Portugal.'

'She came back—with her prize,' he explained dryly.

Rosalind frowned.

'Not Rostrov again?'

He shook his head. 'No, she's improved the company she keeps, I'm glad to say! Her prize—' his voice became even more dry '—is an extremely well-heeled American senior citizen by name of Hiram T. Hackensacker. Apparently, according to Sable—who had dragged him along to the opening of the O'Hanran golf club, where I encountered her— he has three daughters, all of whom are bent on depriving him of, er, fun, in his closing years. Her mission—' his mouth twitched '—is to thwart their miserable plans...'

They exchanged glances, laughter brimming.

'Good old Sable,' said Rosalind.

'Yes, indeed. We must invite her to our wedding.'

Rosalind stilled.

'Wedding?'

He came towards her. Took the coffee mug out of her hand. Replaced it on the kitchen surface. Slid his hands on either side of her head and stood looking down at her, cradling her face.

'Please marry me. Please come back to Spain with me. Please make a family with me. Please—please love me, Rosalind Foster.'

Love shone from her eyes as she answered.

'I already do,' she whispered. 'I already did.' She reached to kiss him. 'And I always will.'

His arms slid down her shoulders, around her waist, and he held her to him, heart to heart, soul to soul.

The setting sun bathed the *castillo* in golden-rose light. Cesar and Rosalind stood in the entrance courtyard, watching the procession of wedding cars wind down the narrow hairpin bends towards the coast. Last of all was a huge white stretch limo that could hardly negotiate the road.

'Do you think his daughters will speak to him again?' murmured Rosalind wonderingly.

'No chance,' Cesar answered. 'They'll be hightailing it to their lawyers to try and get him declared of unsound mind and then they'll probably hire a hitman to take out Sable!'

'Mrs Hiram T. Hackensacker.' Rosalind rolled Sable's new name around her tongue.

Her new husband put his arm around her.

'To think she beat you to a bridegroom, *querida*.' There was amusement in his voice. Sable Hackensacker had been an unforgettable guest at their wedding party that day, wearing a spectacularly short dress and a shopfull of diamonds, lavishly doting on her ancient husband while shamelessly running her eyes over every male guest. She'd been exuberantly enthusiastic about both her and Rosalind's happy endings—even if she had sighed to her with extravagant envy over Cesar's youth and virility compared with her own bridegroom's.

'I noticed the chauffeur was rather good-looking,' Rosalind observed.

'Let's hope he has enough energy to…er…exercise Sable the way she likes,' he replied.

Rosalind leant her head on his shoulder.

'I'm glad for her,' she said simply. 'I'm glad for the whole world today.'

Cesar tightened his embrace.

'I'm more selfish. I'm only glad for us.'

'Us, too,' allowed his bride.

He bent and kissed her lightly.

He looked at her questioningly. 'Are you sure that you want to go to Granada for our honeymoon?'

She nodded, having no doubts. 'Yes. I want to take Michelle to the last place I went when I was happy with Mum. I want to walk around the gardens of the Alhambra and make my peace with the past. Mum had such a sad life—and what chills me to the core…' she took a shuddering breath '…is that I was all set to repeat it with my daughter…'

She took Cesar's hand and held it to her cheek.

'You came for me, as my father never came for my mother. I will have the life my mother never had because of that, and our daughter will have the family I never did. And all because of you, my own dear love.'

She reached to kiss him in the warmth of the Spanish

sun, happiness and gratitude welling through her like a rich, celestial blessing.

He kissed her back, gently at first. And then, as his mouth tasted hers, less gently. As she pressed her body to his she felt desire, deep and passionate, release within her.

His arms slid around her, holding her to him as he lifted his mouth from hers.

'Tell me, my most adored bride, when will our daughter want feeding again?' Cesar enquired, in a deceptively off-hand fashion.

'Oh, I think we've got about an hour,' Rosalind informed him.

He slipped his arms from her shoulders and took her hand instead, leading her indoors.

'Let's see what we can do in an hour, then,' he said. He bent his head, brushing his lips over hers once more. She sighed, and moved against him.

Happiness bathed her. She had everything—everything her heart could desire. Her husband, her daughter—and the whole world was theirs.

Cesar's kiss deepened.

'Let's see,' he said, 'what we can do in a lifetime.'

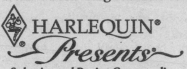

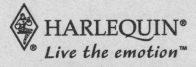

The world's bestselling romance series.

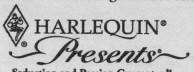

HARLEQUIN® Presents

Seduction and Passion Guaranteed!

THEPRINCESSBRIDES

For duty, for money...for passion!

Discover a thrilling new trilogy from a rising star of Harlequin Presents®, Jane Porter!

Meet the Royals...

Chantal, Nicolette and Joelle are members of the blue-blooded Ducasse family. Step inside their sophisticated and glamorous world and watch as these beautiful princesses find they have to marry three international playboys—for duty, for money... and definitely for passion!

Don't miss

THE SULTAN'S BOUGHT BRIDE (#2418)
September 2004

THE GREEK'S ROYAL MISTRESS (#2424)
October 2004

THE ITALIAN'S VIRGIN PRINCESS (#2430)
November 2004

Pick up a Harlequin Presents® novel and you will enter a world of spine-tingling passion and provocative, tantalizing romance!

Available wherever Harlequin books are sold.

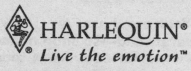

HARLEQUIN®
Live the emotion™

If you enjoyed what you just read,
then we've got an offer you can't resist!

Take 2 bestselling
love stories FREE!
Plus get a FREE surprise gift!

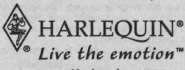

The world's bestselling romance series.

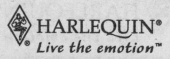

Receive a FREE hardcover book from

H A R L E Q U I N R O M A N C E ®

in September!

Harlequin Romance celebrates the launch of the line's new cover design by offering you this exclusive offer valid only in September, only in Harlequin Romance.

To receive your FREE HARDCOVER BOOK written by bestselling author Emilie Richards, send us four proofs of purchase from any September 2004 Harlequin Romance books. Further details and proofs of purchase can be found in all September 2004 Harlequin Romance books.

Must be postmarked no later than October 31.

Don't forget to be one of the first to pick up a copy of the new-look Harlequin Romance novels in September!

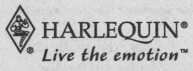

Visit us at www.eHarlequin.com

HRPOP0904